I0658458

Marah Cove

The final volume of the Trevannions' trilogy

Audrey Morris

M.A. Consultants Limited

This edition published in September 2011 by:

M.A. Consultants Limited
11 Belmore Avenue
Pyrford
Woking
Surrey
GU22 8LN

Cover photographs by Mike Morris

ISBN 978-1-903690-03-1

Marah Cove is the final book in the Trevannions' trilogy.

The first book, "The Granite House" (ISBN 1 903690 01 03), and the second "The Unquiet House" (ISBN 978 1 903690 02 1) are also available from M.A. Consultants Limited.

With thanks to all my family and friends with special mention for my husband Mike and to my daughters Frances and Sara for help with proof reading as well as their encouragement.

Synopsis of the Trevannions' Trilogy

Set in Cornwall in the late 1800s the books follow the fortunes of Barnabas Trevannion, his wife Eliza, their five children and other members of the family and friends.

Book One, "The Granite House" covers the meeting of Barnabas and Eliza Talland, their marriage and settling into family life in Roscarne, a granite house set on a Cornish cliff-top. Eliza gives birth to twins, Nathaniel and Caroline, followed in relatively quick succession by three more children, John, Nessa and Joel.

Barnabas' mine, Wheal Eliza, prospers and all appears to be going well until a mine disaster causes closure of the mine and Eliza and the five children have to move to a smaller house, while Barnabas leaves the country to seek his fortune elsewhere.

Book Two, "The Unquiet House" finds Eliza, the children and Uncle Tobias living in much reduced circumstances in a house with a sinister secret.

Following the death of her husband, Sir James Treloyhan, Eliza's sister and her two children come to stay in the already cramped house. Family feuds are forgotten as they deal with a variety of perils, some of which seem to originate in the house itself.

Barnabas returns and all appears to be set fair as the family return to Roscarne.

In this final book in the trilogy, Marah Cove, the saga continues ……..

Characters in the Trevannions' Trilogy

Family at Roscarne:

Barnabas Trevannion – Master of Roscarne
Eliza Trevannion (nee Talland) – Wife of Barnabas
Nathaniel & Caroline – Twins (eldest children)
John, Nessa & Joel – other children of Barnabas and Eliza
Tobias – Barnabas' Uncle
Grace – Eliza's Sister
Richard & Elestren – Grace's children
Ewella – Barnabas's Sister

The Manor:

Austol Treloyhan – Lord of the Manor
Eulalia – Wife of Austol
Kenwyn – Eldest Son of Austol
Lamorna – Eldest Daughter of Austol
Melwyn, Kerra, Elowen, and the triplets, Cryda, Tegen and Caja – Other Daughters of Austol
Edgar – Eulalia's Brother (Austol's Brother-in-Law)

Other Characters:

Aunt Gloria – Eliza's and Grace's Aunt
Yelland Conyers – Husband of Gloria
Rose – Friend of Eliza
Seth Quinn – Husband of Rose
Jael – Friend of Eliza; Mistress Annie – Jael's Mother
Nicholas & Morwenna Tregadillett – Minister & Wife
Henry Pauncefoot – Animal Doctor
Selena – Friend of Barnabas
Jean Luc – Painter
Mathey – Groundsman
Mrs Adwyn – Cook; Hedra – Nanny; Miss Maisie – Teacher

1

The rain began at dawn. At first it just whispered against the windows and only sleepless Eliza heard it. By midday it had become a brutal torrent assaulting Roscarne, battering the windows and walls, an enraged enemy turning the day into twilight. Water cascaded from every gutter, pooling on the lawns till the house appeared marooned in water. Barnabas Trevannion, master of the house, decided to wait for some diminution of the downpour before he ventured out. The new governess, Miss Maisie, evidently not from Cornwall, fluttered from window to window declaring that she had never seen anything like it before. Ewella found satisfaction in telling her about the flooding at Carnglaze, with suitable embellishments, insinuating that this storm was nothing and she should see what the weather was like in winter.

'She'll leave before the winter!' whispered Joel. 'Look at her face!' Nessa frowned at him.

'It's unkind to tease her so. You know perfectly well that we have lovely blue days in both the autumn and the winter and it can be quite warm.' Joel shrugged.

Eliza, meanwhile had repaired to her small room at the top of the house, ostensibly to do some sewing, but in reality wanting some time to think. Roscarne was the place she loved. Outwardly it was still the ruggedly handsome house surrounded by vistas of sea and sky that had captivated her for so many years previously but inside the granite walls the atmosphere had changed. Barnabas, an enthusiastic business man in the tin mining industry, engaged in using the money he had made in Australia to reopen his mines and equip them with the latest in pumping gear, at the same time reforming the consortium he had headed previously, was seldom at home. When he was, Eliza reflected bitterly, he was remote, treating her politely as if she were a guest. Even Ewella, his sister, noticed the difference in him and made barbed comments about the way men treated their wives after a long time together. 'But we were not together,' thought Eliza. 'He was in Australia and I was in Carnglaze with all the family. Carnglaze! A haunted house no less! And I have not forgiven him for that!'

Eliza tried to overcome her feelings of neglect by escaping when she could to this little room at the top of the house, a room once readied for the new governess but now required by the mistress. There she could gaze out at the sea, enjoying all its moods and ignoring the sewing she had brought. There she could muse upon the changes in her life and formulate plans for the house, for her children, for her close friends. It was there she felt the loosening of bonds that tied her down and the first intimations of freedom – freedom of the mind if not the body. It was only when she began sleeping in the little single bed, lulled by the winds outside, did Barnabas protest.

'Eliza, you need to move back to our room,' he requested, in cold tones. 'What will the servants –and others – think?' Not a line of reasoning to appeal to his wife.

'So concerned about the opinions of other people?' she said, her voice deceptively mild. 'I would have thought it was because you wanted me near you. I see I was wrong.' Her taunt left Barnabas shaken. He was not used to having his decisions questioned and he realised that he had given unwitting offence to his wife. He was well aware that with the demands of the day roiling through his mind he would come to bed late and exhausted. Then sleep would fall upon him, heavy as floodwater, leaving Eliza to toss and turn beside him, aware that again he was far away from her.

The children were another bone of contention. Sixteen year old Nathaniel and fourteen year old John were attending a boarding school near Exeter but when Barnabas wanted to dispatch Joel to the same place, Eliza proved obstinate. It was not often she defied the wishes of her husband but this time she was adamant. Joel would receive his education at the hands of Miss Maisie, the new governess, alongside his sisters, Caroline and Nessa and Grace's children, Richard and Elestren. Barnabas had offered to pay for Richard to attend boarding school but Grace had refused.

'I like to keep my children close,' she said sweetly.

'I cannot believe she said that!' erupted Ewella when she heard. 'She does nothing for them! Poor Nanny Hannah is still running after them although they are far too old to have a nanny! But then Barnabas has always let Grace have her own way.'

Eliza bit her lip. She would have liked to join in Ewella's tirade even though her feelings about her sister had softened somewhat. Still angry about Grace having deceived her with Barnabas, she was however, sorry for her. Her husband's premature death, the scandal surrounding Richard's birth and bouts of ill health had not made her sister's life easy. Now she floated about the house in a variety of decorative dresses, ignoring Ewella's poorly hidden disapproval, occasionally demanding plaintively that she needed fresh air and would Mathey harness the cart. She seemed to have forgotten that now they had a new carriage and a smart pony and trap. No, she only remembered the cart from their Carnglaze days. This worried Eliza. Would Grace relapse into her shadowy half world again, a world in which her husband, James Treloyhan was still alive and Austol the usurper of his title? Grace, angry and difficult as she could be, nevertheless had times of a sweet eagerness to please. But when trapped in her muddled world, striking out at everyone, desperately trying to make sense of what was happening to her, she was not easy to manage. Poor Richard bore the brunt of her moods and now, at ten years old, was also growing up. His younger sister, Elestren, a clone of her mother in appearance but vastly different in temperament, looked to Richard for protection. Grace seemed to have no maternal feelings for Elestren and had been known to berate the poor girl for existing at all.

'She doesn't mean it, you know,' Richard assured his sister. 'Mama has had much grief in her life. She gets cross and says things without thinking.'

The rain had been falling for four days but at last it showed signs of easing. A freakish wind blew the clouds into rags and allowed patches of clear sky to appear. Grace, who had been flitting through the house like an angry butterfly, saw her chance to go outside.

'Surely Mistress Grace, you won't go out like that!' said Ewella, trapping her at the door. 'You have no wrap and look at your shoes!'

'Don't fuss, Ewella!' snapped Grace, looking at her brocade slippers as if they did not belong to her. 'I shall not be outside for long. But I need fresh air!' And she slipped through the door.

'Mama – would you like me to accompany you?' It was Richard, always weighted by a burden of anxiety about her.

'I do not need a keeper!' retorted Grace. 'You would be better occupied looking after Elestren. She needs help with her numbers!' Without turning her head, she marched off down the path that led to the sea, her gauzy dress blowing wildly and her blonde hair escaping from its pins. Richard sighed heavily and turned back into the house. Why could he never please his mother?

By mid-afternoon the clouds were gone and the blue of the sky was intense.

'Where IS Grace?' asked Eliza. 'She has missed lunch again.'

'She went out,' volunteered Joel. 'Walking.'

'Walking!' exclaimed Caroline. 'That's not like her. And the ground is sodden.'

8

'She'll come back when she is wet enough,' said Ewella acidly. 'I warned her but she took no notice. She will get bronchitis at the very least.'

'I'll go and look for her,' decided Eliza. 'Richard, would you like to come with me? And I think we should wear gumboots. The path outside still looks more like a stream.'

There was no sign of Grace in the garden at the back of the house which faced out to sea. This was a relief as the garden was edged by a steep cliff which fell vertically to the sand of Marietta Cove far below. The children were not allowed there alone and Eliza had the feeling that the same should apply to Grace. Slippery as a fish she could veer from one mood to another, from one reasonable time to an episode of unreason that could have serious consequences, as when her obsessive belief that Austol had deprived James of his title to the Manor had contributed to Eulalia's illness and subsequent death. And Eliza was sure that in her right mind she would not treat Richard as she did.

There was nothing else for it. They would have to descend to the beach. In single file they followed the steep, twisting path as it wound downwards, negotiating the slippery patches with care. Neither spoke, each trying to extinguish the spark of worry that always accompanied Grace's excursions. There was no sign of her in Marietta Cove or along the stretch of beach beyond to Marah Cove. It was hardly likely she would have attempted to climb Marah Cliffs which reared ahead.

'She has probably gone to wander round the rhododendron garden,' said Eliza, unaccountably relieved. 'We shall go to look there.' They were about to turn back to the path when a sudden subterranean rumbling caused Eliza to clutch Richard's arm. Horrified, they saw earth and rock on the cliff ahead of them begin to move, then gather momentum and slide down to the beach below with a rushing and crashing of soil and stones, leaving a raw scar on the cliff face and a pile of rubble at its foot.

'But – Mama?' faltered Richard. 'Do you think ....?'
'She would not leave the path to climb on the cliff!'
said his aunt comfortingly. 'But I must go back and tell
Barnabas before he goes out again. Come quickly, Richard.'
     'Nothing to worry about,' said Barnabas. 'The cliffs
are granite and not prone to serious landslides. But the rain
has been fierce – I expect that caused it. Jed and I will have a
closer look when it is drier.' With that, Eliza had to be
content. But the incident made her thoughtful. Was it an
omen?

     'She's here!' announced Ewella, animosity in her
tone. 'She came sauntering in fairly soon after you left –and
gave me the brocade slippers to dry out and clean. Mistress
Grace, I am NOT a servant girl, I said to her but she just gave
me that maddening but I know you will do it smile and swept
off!'
     'I shall have a word with her, Ewella,' said Eliza.
'But you know that she does not always think straight.'
     'Not when it suits her, that's true.'
     'W – where did she go, Ewella?' asked Richard. 'I
thought she might have been caught in the landslide...'
     'Don't you worry, Master Richard! She's fine!' said
Ewella rather tartly. Did Grace realise what a caring son she
had? The adoration shone out of his face when he looked at
her but it was an adoration unrecognised and unreturned.
Childless Ewella had a soft spot for Richard and Grace's
careless treatment of him made her angry.

Just then Uncle Tobias hobbled in from his study, his
drooping whiskers and untidy hair making him look like a
lugubrious gnome.
     'Barnabas is wrong!' he croaked. 'Landslides do
occur on granite cliffs – and more often than supposed. The
zawn between here and Hellesveor was caused by an
enormous fall of rock back in the late 1700s – '
     'Why did it happen?' Richard was intrigued.

'Nobody really knows but there were rumours of an earthquake. Also there were reports that mining activity could have caused it. Guess-work, really.' Uncle Tobias shrugged his shoulders.

'Now, Ewella, any of that saffron cake you made left for me?'

2

'Mistress Eliza, Lord Treloyhan has come to call.' Eliza sighed. She had been sitting at the desk in the drawing room, trying to make sense of the household accounts and she disliked being interrupted. Particularly she disliked the enforced contact she had so often with Austol Treloyhan. He professed a deep friendship for her – which was not so on her part – and an admiration for her advice on subjects varying from Grace, her children, Richard and Elestren, Kenwyn, his son, any one of his seven daughters and anyone else he could think of in his circle of relations and acquaintances.

'Mistress Eliza. I am pleased to find you home.' He brought with him the scent of cologne, of fine cigars, his hair appeared oiled and his whiskers were immaculate. Tall, and, it must be said, still rather intimidating, he took Eliza's hand and held it with unnecessary pressure. Only his eyes were still cold as quartz, cold enough to send a shiver down Eliza's back.

'I am so sorry but Barnabas is at Wheal Eliza and Grace is confined to her room with a megrim,' she stumbled.

'No matter. It is really you I come to see, dear Eliza. I value the perspective you give me on the various problems that are tormenting me. Since the death of my dear wife Eulalia I have no one to turn to – no one that I trust,' he added.

'Surely your brother-in-law Edgar....?'

'No. Since his terrifying experiences at Carnglaze, he has not been the same person. I would not wish to undermine his stability further.'

'I do understand that,' Eliza admitted, remembering that dreadful night when poor Edgar had been taken over by the wandering spirit belonging to Samuel Hooper, the smuggler, and, as a result, being forced also to suffer Samuel's terrible remorse for causing the death of his wife. A dreadful nightmarish time that seemed so far away now she was enfolded by the security of Roscarne. At times, she could hardly believe what had happened in that dreadful house. So many children in the one comfortless room, lying side by side like pilchards in a box. Then the arrival of Grace and her children and nanny to add to the crowding in that house. Worst of all was the eerie atmosphere, the ghosts, sometimes sobbing, sometimes singing, then the floods....It had not been a peaceful time and she was thankful it was behind them. Austol coughed, breaking into her reverie.

'Of course I realise how busy Barnabas must be just now – and I have no need to see Mistress Grace at the moment. I am pleased that you are here,' he said.

'I shall ring for tea,' said Eliza, unwillingly.

A discussion ensued concerning Caja, the youngest of his daughters. Then Austol leaned back in his chair and heaved a deep sigh. Eliza wondered if he was coming to the most important part of his visit.

'Lamorna!' he uttered, with emphasis. Eliza looked enquiring. 'All she wants to do is draw and paint. When she has assignments to do for her governess, where do I find her? Up in the attic with an overall on and paint all over the place. She tells me that she wishes to go to London to attend an art college and is not interested in any academic subject I might suggest.' It seemed to Eliza that the rejection of advice from her father was what rankled most in Austol's mind.

'Is she good? I mean does she have any talent?'

'Considering she has had no tuition she seems very competent. But I will not allow her to go to London. She is only fourteen!'

'Then that is the end of the matter, surely. She will do as you say?'

'She is very strong willed,' admitted Austol gloomily. 'I am interested in art myself – portrait painting in particular – but it is only a hobby. Lamorna declares that she intends to make it her career. She says she will not marry and spend her time raising a brood of children and pandering to some selfish husband. Where does she get these outlandish ideas?' Eliza had a good idea where those ideas originated but decided to keep quiet. She hoped that would be all. But no. With an abrupt change of subject he leaned forward.

'And Seth Quinn? Is he still involved in the consortium?'

She was caught by surprise and felt the colour rising in her cheeks. Austol did not make random comments. There was some purpose to this.

'I believe so,' she said cautiously.

'And of course you do see him regularly – married to your friend Rose is he not?'

Eliza was puzzled. He knew perfectly well that was so. What did he want? He was not inclined to enlighten her, sitting back in his chair and changing the subject but those cold eyes never left her face. She felt she was in the sights of a predator who was tracking her down with merciless precision. But why? She was a thirty five year old matron with five children, married to the owner of Roscarne. Why was Austol so interested in her? As Barnabas was hoping to inveigle Austol into his consortium, more for his contacts than his money, Eliza resisted the temptation to show him out with all speed. With her husband's return from overseas, she had hoped that there would be a reduction in Austol's obsessive interest in her and a lessening of his constant attentions but that did not seem to be happening. Lamorna, she felt, was just an excuse.

'Just the person I wanted to see!' Uncle Tobias rescued her from her uncomfortable meeting by shuffling in and insisting that Austol should come and inspect the maps he had acquired from a local archive. 'Some interesting information about the Manor,' he beamed. Eliza made good her escape but not before Austol invited – demanded – her presence for supper – with Barnabas and Uncle Tobias of course. It was unlikely that Barnabas would spare the time but at least she would have her uncle with her.

Up in her little room, she gazed out at a bland grey sea, so calm it seemed painted. But her own calm had vanished with the mention of Seth Quinn. Even the sound of his name had the power to cause turmoil within her. Seth Quinn, he of the flopping black hair and the dark eyes that seemed to see to her very soul, his sharp angled face which softened when he looked at her. She could remember his impressive display when he fought the big negro at Lanteglos winter fair and then his kindness to her when she was taken ill, her baby on the way. She remembered how he had rescued her on the Morvah Road after she had run away from Barnabas. After that it seemed that care for her was always foremost until the shock of his proposal to Rose, her companion and friend, an event which weakened their friendship and rocked Eliza's feelings for him. It WAS a mistake, she assured herself, based on a misunderstanding – but then what real difference did it make? She herself was married to Barnabas and could not leave her children to follow a dream. So why could she not accept the pattern her life had woven round her and be content?

A knock on the door. It was Ewella, always the glad bringer of bad tidings.

'Mistress Maisie is having trouble with Joel again,' she announced. 'Apparently he ran away from his lessons this afternoon and when she finally tracked him down he kicked her! Then he told the new cook that her pastry was so heavy that he couldn't swallow it, said it was like eating bricks. And him only six years old!'

'Oh dear! He will have hurt Mrs. Adwyn's feelings again. He did not like her hevvacake either!'

'Perhaps he needs discipline – more discipline – ' said Ewella darkly, knowing that she was treading on dangerous ground. Her brother and his spirited wife had clashed on the same subject before.

'Thank you, Ewella. I shall discuss the matter with Barnabas. But Joel IS only six years old.'

Eliza tried to return to her former thoughts but Ewella had disturbed her and she gave up. She decided she would check on the children in the schoolroom before she did anything else. Miss Maisie, conscientious but fluttery and too easily diverted, often needed help, with Joel in particular, but Caroline and Nessa merited the highest praise for their work, Caroline in her aloof and other worldly way and Nessa, so smiley and eager to please. The schoolroom was peaceful, however, so Eliza proceeded to the kitchen where Mrs. Adwyn was making squab pies, watched by Ewella. An awkward silence fell when Eliza appeared and she guessed that she had been the subject of discussion. She looked enquiringly at Ewella, knowing well that lady could not keep a secret.

'News about Seth Quinn – he's bringing Mistress Rose back to Penzance – well before time! Seems the travelling did not help her!' Ewella could not wait to impart the gossip.

'Oh, poor Rose!' cried Eliza. She knew that Seth had taken Rose on a tour of Europe to help her forget the sadness of the several miscarriages she had endured and, it was hoped, to improve her general health. So they had returned. Eliza's concern for Rose did not stop her heart missing a beat when she thought of Seth, just a few miles away in Penzance. Would he come to call soon? Would he bring Rose or would she be too fragile? She was conscious of Ewella staring at her, trying to assess her reaction.

'This is sad news,' she said. 'But I am sure we shall see them soon and can offer our help. Perhaps you could prepare some of those chicken dishes you do so well, Mrs. Adwyn? I know that Rose was very partial to them.'

'Oh yes, Mistress Eliza.' Mrs. Adwyn was pleased.

Eliza found Barnabas in his study – rare indeed for him to be at home during the day. He was shuffling sheaves of paper on his desk, his forehead screwed into a myriad wrinkles. Not a good time to tackle him about a visit to the Manor.

'I am afraid that will not be convenient,' he declared curtly. 'You and Tobias will have to go without me.'

'I should prefer not to go at all,' said Eliza.' I am tired of Austol's constant visits here and I do NOT want to go to the Manor.'

'Eliza, please!' Barnabas was irritable. 'I do not wish to offend him. Please go and make my apologies. I am sure you will enjoy it – you will see Edgar after all.' His voice had taken on a heavily jocular note. 'And Uncle Tobias will love it. He has too few outings in his life.'

Eliza realised that she had no hope of changing his mind but she made one last try.

'Barnabas – you and I have not been out together for so long! I should value your company – '

'Another time! Do not whine, Eliza. Now, I have work to do.'

Seething, Eliza left him. The only consolation was that Barnabas appeared to think that Edgar was an attraction for her. Not Seth!

That Barnabas could not come to the Manor did not disturb Austol. He welcomed Eliza and Tobias with great geniality, announcing that it was his pleasure to invite his son, Kenwyn, to the supper table and, of course, Edgar. Eliza was relieved that the quarrels between father and son appeared to have been resolved, finding Kenwyn much subdued and his aversion to his father moderated. He listened politely to the conversation and offered a few comments, the perfect son of the host. Edgar, however, was a worry. He looked gaunt and pale and his hands were shaking. Something was still sadly amiss with the poor man. She said as much to Austol who had insisted that she take a walk with him through the gardens in the twilight summer evening.

'I feel that I am partially responsible,' said Austol gravely. 'I did suggest to him that it might be better if he left Cornwall and all its sad memories behind him and returned to Devon but he insisted that he wished to keep on his work as a Preventive man and continue to stay here.'

'You will allow him that?' said Eliza.

'Of course, dear Eliza, if you so advise it.'

'It is not for me to advise anything!' declared Eliza. 'But you are his nearest relative and he has been at home here for so long!'

'I shall do as you wish,' said Austol, hiding a smile.

3

'Jael! How lovely to see you! I had no idea you were coming back so soon!' A delighted Eliza held out her hands to her visitor and drew her to a comfortable chair. 'Have you been successful selling your medicines and potions at the fairs?' And where is Mistress Annie?'

'One question at a time,' laughed Jael. 'Everything has been going very well. Mother has gone to stay with a friend in Penzance for a few days and I was wondering if I could stay with you for a little while?'

'Nothing would please me better! I have missed you. Without you and Rose here I have no one to turn to for advice – or for interesting gossip!'

Jael looked shrewdly at her one time mistress, a mistress who had become a good friend after the trials they had endured at Carnglaze. She noted that Eliza, while still comely at thirty five, her dark hair glossy, her deep blue eyes lively, nevertheless had a sad droop to her mouth. She had lost weight which had sharpened her features and there was little trace of the sunny, plump young girl she had been.

'A flower touched with frost,' was Jael's thought. Not what she expected. Eliza and her children were reunited with Barnabas and safe within the granite walls of Roscarne – why should she look like that? No doubt about it, the impulse to visit Roscarne had been a wise one. Something was amiss.

For her part, Eliza was scrutinising Jael. Gossip labelled her as the daughter of a witch even though her mother, Mistress Annie, denied this, insisting she was not a witch, merely a pellar – a wandering wise woman who concocted medicines and simple charms. However she admitted that she and her daughter both were often in danger from irate farmers who blamed them for the ills that befell their cattle or from those who found that the love potion they had been given did not work. The demands for their skills were many and secret but failures meant mother and daughter were subject to threats and chased away. Jael took these risks as one of the setbacks of her kind of life but finding new cures for illnesses and new herbs to use spurred her on, finding great satisfaction in making discoveries that helped people and animals. She had changed little in the last few years – still slight with pale blonde hair, the luminous quality of her skin showing no signs of the time she spent on the road and those slanting silvery eyes observing the world around her.

'Jael – I do not believe you came here just by accident,' said Eliza suddenly. 'Do you have a special reason?'

'Do I have to have a reason?' parried Jael, frowning slightly.

'No, of course not – but you did say you would be away for at least a year.'

'I was worried – I heard that Seth and Rose are back in Penzance – '

'Yes.' Eliza's voice was bleak.

'But that's not all. I admit I have been feeling uneasy for you – for all of you. Just like Caroline said once – the day is warm and bright but a black bar of cloud has appeared on the horizon.'

Eliza glanced out of the window.

'It is a bright blue day outside,' she said, trying to hide the tremor in her voice. She remembered only too well that Jael could sense what others could not. And Caroline was following in her footsteps.

'The last thing I want to do is alarm you,' said Jael, hastily, aware that she had done exactly that. 'But I feel so close to you and your family. Besides, I missed you. Now I shall go and see Ewella and Uncle Tobias – I don't suppose Barnabas is here?'

'Never is,' said Eliza, briefly. 'The girls and Joel and Richard are in the schoolroom with Miss Maisie for their lessons. Caroline especially will be delighted to see you. She moped after you had gone so this will be a nice surprise for her.'

Supper that evening was a cheerful affair. For once Barnabas did come home and exerted himself to be welcoming and charming, professing himself to have missed her presence at Roscarne. Grace also joined them at dinner, a little vague but in one of her sweeter moods, while Ewella was gratified to learn that Mistress Annie had asked to be remembered to her especially. Uncle Tobias did not appear; apparently his legs ached more than usual and he was unwilling to leave his bed.

'Changes in the weather upset him,' declared Barnabas, briskly. 'I shall join him later for a nightcap.'
Eliza glanced out of the window, but there were no clouds. It was a peaceful evening, the blue of the sky shading into mauve and pink as the sun set and the wind seeming soft as rose petals. She sighed. Why were so many beautiful days marred by troubles and worries that popped up like the stones in her vegetable garden? But their days at Carnglaze had been far worse. Problems there had been serious. She should stop worrying and just enjoy being back in Roscarne.

'I do think, Mama, that I should be allowed to take supper with you in the evening,' Caroline suggested hopefully. 'After all, I am sixteen now. Not a child anymore.'
They were all gathered in the drawing room, listening to Jael and chatting desultorily. Eliza hesitated. It was a thought that had crossed her mind previously but she feared her husband's reaction and she did not want to start such a discussion in front of Jael. Barnabas was not reasonable when it came to the 'discipline' of his children. To her surprise he leaned back in his chair and nodded.

21

'I think that would be quite suitable,' he agreed. 'Perhaps I should tell you that Austol has made a similar suggestion with regard to his eldest girl – '
'And she is only fourteen!' said Caroline eagerly.
'We shall invite Austol and his daughter – Lamorna, I think is her name, for a special supper,' her father said. 'It will be good training for you both.' Eliza was silent. Again, no discussion, just a decision made with no reference to her opinion. Ewella smiled, a sanctimonious smile. She approved of the times when her brother asserted his authority.

Later that night, Eliza lay in the bedroom she and Barnabas shared, staring gloomily into the darkness. She felt hemmed in by the heavy dark furniture that she could feel rather than see and the velvet curtains which separated her from the window and the night sky. Even the bedclothes seemed to be weighing her down and keeping her a prisoner. So Barnabas was back. Yes. And still she was waiting for him, knowing that she would not sleep until he, too, came to bed. Jael, of course, recognised that the household was not running smoothly even though Barnabas had made such efforts to be charming. She would have noticed that he never referred to his wife when making decisions; this man was not the Barnabas of before. Prior to his flight to Australia after the closure of the Trevannion mines, he had been a reasonable, loving man, authoritarian it was true, but no more than any other husband and master of a household. What had happened to change him so?

And how uncaring of Nessa's feelings he had been, when she complained that she would be left with Joel, like a baby in the nursery. Her big eyes had brimmed with tears but her father had ignored her. So unfair to the usually smiling and obedient little girl who was so eager to please. Somehow, Roscarne, the house she loved and had longed for, had not worked its usual magic on their return and she did not feel safe, she felt uneasy. A picture of the crumbling cliff, stones and soil loosened and falling, slipped into her mind's eye, adding to her feeling of insecurity, her feeling that the ground beneath her feet was unsafe.

Then there was Austol. Always Austol in the background. She did not understand him and was uncomfortably aware that, when in the same room, his eyes never left her. He was adept at finding excuses to visit Roscarne or to invite her to the Manor and she felt constrained to do so, aware that Barnabas wished it. More and more she felt a sacrificial victim waiting for the sea beast that was Austol and in need of her own Perseus to come to her rescue.

Jael stayed for several days, to Caroline's particular delight, and the weather stayed calm and warm so they were able to take walks along the beach and the cliffs. Nothing untoward transpired and Eliza began to relax. Jael uttered no more warnings and it was only when Barnabas insisted on inviting Austol and his eldest daughter, Lamorna, to supper at Roscarne that she decided it was time to rejoin her mother in Penzance.

     'Austol is not one of my favourite people,' she admitted to Eliza. 'I don't know what it is about him but he sets my teeth on edge. You take care, Eliza. Don't trust him.'

     'I'm with you there,' said Eliza. 'But come to see us again and don't leave it too long. Please give my regards to Mistress Annie and I wish you both, good luck in your travels.' She tried to sound cheerful but as Mathey drove away with Jael to Penzance, she felt that she was losing the one real friend she had.

Loneliness lurked in the corners of Roscarne. At one time she had felt so secure with Barnabas and her friend Rose – but now? Rose was married to Seth Quinn and her feelings for her one time friend were tarnished. Seth – at last she could say his name. He had declared his love for her and then had married Rose and whisked her off to Arizona where he intended to develop his gold mine. She had to admit that he had made an honourable choice. Barnabas was still her husband even though he was miles away in Australia. She remembered how she had willed Seth to stay but he had escaped the temptation and fulfilled his promise to Rose, a promise immediately regretted once given.

She scuttled up to her special room and threw herself into the armchair by the window, staring with unseeing eyes at the sea. Seth filled her mind and her thoughts and she longed for him with an intensity that frightened her. Gradually the room darkened. A black line of cloud separated sea and sky at the horizon, promising storms to come and a veil of gauzy cloud drifted over the sun. Sighing, Eliza decided she had better check on the children and then visit Mrs. Adwyn to see how the preparations for supper were progressing. She half hoped that a real storm would prevent their visitors from coming but of course that would only postpone the unwelcome event.

The storm was still threatening when Austol and Lamorna arrived, he immaculate as ever and his daughter in a pretty dress of pale green silk with fine lace at her throat and her hair up in curls threaded with white ribbon. Her dress was at odds with her sharp features and wary expression.

'Her colour sense is all her own,' Austol said, in response to Eliza's compliments. 'Not like Eulalia's at all.' This last was in an undertone as Caroline and Lamorna greeted each other and were soon chatting easily. Perhaps this supper had been a good idea after all, Eliza reflected. Caroline missed her twin brother, Nathaniel, and Lamorna was nearer her age than Nessa. Barnabas watched the girls with approval, then engaged Austol and Uncle Tobias in a discussion of local tin mining problems. At last Eliza could relax. She, in her turn, chatted to Ewella and the supper passed without incident. As Eliza and Barnabas bade farewell to their guests, Austol suggested that he would like to host a supper the following week.

'I have a particular reason,' he said. 'Lamorna here has been painting and I should like your opinion as to her talent. She wishes to go to London to an art school but I am uncertain that this would be in her best interests.' Lamorna flushed with anger.

'Father! My paintings are not ready to show anyone! How could you!'

'I think that is so exciting!' Caroline interrupted. Always quick to respond to the feelings of others, she contrived to divert Austol's annoyance at his daughter's response.

'My brother, Nathaniel, can draw. His letters are full of illustrations but he says there is no time for art at school and I think that is a pity.'

'It is such a talent,' agreed Eliza. 'I was always impressed by his biology notes and the drawings with them. Do not worry, Lamorna, we shall only look at the paintings you want to show us.' This did not seem to please Austol but she received a look of gratitude from Lamorna as he hustled her away.

'I'm glad Austol is not my father,' Caroline whispered to Eliza.

4

The promised storm had not materialised. It had drifted menacingly up country, leaving the sun to come out again, lighting up the coast of north Cornwall with an autumn glow. Eliza, Caroline and Uncle Tobias presented themselves at the Manor, minus the presence of Barnabas who cited work as his excuse.

Lamorna, Austol's eldest daughter, was waiting to greet them, dressed this time in sombre grey twill with a sullen expression to match. Eliza wondered if this was a protest against her father who had disregarded her wishes and insisted he would show her paintings. Her expression darkened even more when Austol appeared, exuding a bonhomie that Eliza felt did not suit him.

'I am looking forward to showing you Lamorna's recent paintings,' he said. 'I should welcome your views. Lamorna, my dear – please take Mistress Eliza and Caroline up to the attic while I talk business with Tobias. I shall join you later.'

A silent Lamorna led the way up several flights of stairs and down a long corridor. The door at the end, wooden and heavy, creaked open and they found themselves in a room flooded with light from large windows and skylights. Canvases were piled at one end, faces to the wall, apart from two which had been placed on an easel in the middle of the room. The first was of a fisherman with a weather-beaten face, sitting on a rock, staring out to sea, a sea that was turbulent and uninviting.

'That's so good,' said Caroline, breaking the silence. 'I saw a similar painting sent to that artist in Rosmorren, the one who is opening his house to sell pictures – I forget his name.'

'You mean he is opening a gallery?' exclaimed Lamorna, suddenly animated.

'I believe so. Jael told me and when she was here we went to have a look. There is not much space and he only has a few pictures there but apparently they were all painted from life. They are of fishermen and servant girls and ordinary people. Quite different from the usual grand paintings full of cherubs and bare ladies!'

'I did not know you had taken an interest in art!' Eliza could not help interrupting.

'I think, Mama, there is quite a lot you do not know about me!' Caroline smiled. 'Before Professor Martineau retired he talked to us about classical painters, and another group called the Impressionists but unfortunately John was bored – you know how John can be! So we soon returned to maths and science.' At this, Lamorna snorted in a rather unladylike way.

'Boys!' she said, with scorn.

'I like this one,' Eliza studied the second painting. 'That could be Mrs. Kershaw, our former cook, sitting at the kitchen table, peeling potatoes.'

'I did that,' said Lamorna, with pride. 'Our cook let me paint her in our kitchen – so long as my father did not get to know!'

'And what was it that you kept from your father?' Austol had insinuated himself into the room, unnoticed by his daughter and visitors.

'Er – I have been trying to paint people from life!' blurted Lamorna, avoiding the question. 'The results are more realistic than painting from memory or posing them ....'

'Of course. But why choose an ancient fisherman? And a cook? Surely you could find a more attractive subject? Flowers – or trees – or a pretty girl?'

'Austol, you have a very talented daughter.' Eliza said, hastily. 'Look at the lines on the old man's face – and his expression. It tells a story. He wants to go to sea but has become aware that he is getting old and it is too rough for him. At least that is what the picture says to me.' Lamorna stared at Eliza.

'That is exactly what I wanted to show,' she said. 'How clever of you, Mistress Eliza! I hoped to make it clear that words are not always necessary.'

'And you have succeeded,' smiled Eliza. 'It seems to me, Austol,' she turned to him and said bravely 'Lamorna would indeed benefit from Art School. I venture to say that even though I have seen only two of her works.'

Clearly Austol was taken aback at this unstinted praise.

'I value your opinion, of course, dear Eliza. But she should not go to an Art school in London! That is what she wants! Would you approve of someone as young as Lamorna being exposed to the dangers of a big city? Surely not!'

'Perhaps there is somewhere in Truro or Penzance…..?' Eliza was aware that Lamorna was scowling and the tension between father and daughter was growing.

'Or even Newlyn,' said Caroline. 'I hear that artists have come from France and other parts of England to paint there….'

'London would be better,' sulked Lamorna. Her father glared at her.

'I am delighted that your talent is appreciated. But you are only fourteen – '

'Nearly fifteen!' interrupted his daughter. He ignored that. 'London is out of the question! Mistress Eliza, here, agrees with me.' On the point of a heated denial, Eliza realised that it would only anger Austol to refute that statement. The temperature needed to be lowered.

'Perhaps you should make enquiries? It would be so good for Lamorna to have some help and guidance – perhaps nearer to home?' Eliza knew she was on dangerous ground. Austol was not one to take interference easily but it seemed that he allowed her to say what she liked, reinforcing the feeling that he was treating her with special care. Why?

'We shall talk further,' Austol said. 'Now I have to leave you ladies for the moment. But we shall convene for tea in half an hour.'

Lamorna made sure that Austol had indeed left them. Then she pulled out a canvas and placed it defiantly on the easel. And waited.

'What fantastic colours!' exclaimed Caroline, breaking an extended and shocked silence. The canvas was in oil, a swirl of blues and greens. There were no shapes or figures but the colours seemed to fight their way out of the canvas if they were living. The message was of anger, a barely repressed anger. Eliza stood in silence for a moment, absorbing the impact of the painting.

'Lamorna, my dear, you have painted moods and feelings so that you make us sense them,' she said, quietly. 'I know nothing about the rules for good painting but I feel that you have more than an ordinary talent. This picture of yours has such strength that those feelings are communicated to us.' Lamorna turned red and then white and seemed too overcome to say a word. Caroline, however, burst out enthusiastically. 'This is so much more interesting! Have you done any more?'

'Not like that,' said Lamorna.' I woke up one morning and just had to paint what I felt! That's the only one. Now this is what my father really likes.' She showed them a water colour of a pretty girl trying on a necklace, a decorative picture but one without the mesmeric power of the previous canvas.

'Did you do that?' Caroline was puzzled. Lamorna laughed contemptuously

'Oh yes. My father is collecting paintings and I know exactly what he likes. I hoped that if I pleased him he would let me go to London. I know that it is a feeble picture – Oh dear – ' she stopped.

Eliza was feeling more and more awkward during Lamorna's outburst. She was not yet fifteen and should not be speaking about her father in such a way.

'I had no idea that your father was so interested in art,' she began, just as Austol came in, carrying a large bouquet of hothouse flowers.

'More than interested, my dear Eliza!' he exclaimed. 'I collect portraits for the gallery I am hoping to set up. I expect Lamorna has told you. But I digress. It is your opinion of Lamorna's talent that is important to me.' Eliza was able to assure him that she thought Lamorna had considerable aptitude, sugaring the pill by adding that obviously the talent had come down to her through the family – from her father perhaps?

'I have no special qualifications to judge paintings,' she warned but at least her tactful words had erased the grim expression on Austol's face.

'I am pleased that you think she has some facility in art,' Austol began, returning to the subject that was at the forefront of his mind. 'But perhaps you will agree with me that it is perhaps not advisable for a young girl to be exposed to the vicissitudes of London at such a tender age?'

'I cannot possibly comment!' said Eliza, stifling her wish to do just that.

'Lamorna, perhaps you and Caroline could alert Mrs. Laity that we are coming down for tea, shortly? And these flowers, for you, dear Eliza – the gardener saw you were here and picked them especially. I had asked him of course. Thank you, girls.' It was a clear dismissal. Exchanging grimaces, the two girls did as they were told, leaving an uncomfortable Eliza with Austol.

'Please come with me. I have something else to show you.' He led the way up a flight of narrow stairs to another of the Manor's many attic rooms, this one being smaller but equally well lit with skylights.

'These rooms at the top were servants' quarters in James' time,' he said. 'But with some alterations, we have let in more light. I use one for Lamorna and this one for my collection. I have hopes of opening a proper gallery – perhaps in Rosmorren or even Truro.'

Eliza looked around in disbelief. The walls were lined with portraits, some in watercolours, some sketched in charcoal but most in oil. And they were good. Even though her experience in judging works of art was limited, she recognised that Lamorna had underestimated her father's taste.

Several more canvases lay stacked against the wall but Austol did not offer to show them to her. He stood by and watched her reactions, pleased with the interest on his guest's face.

At teatime, presided over by an avuncular Austol, the chatter from his other daughters precluded any more artistic discussion. However, the sedate little gathering was interrupted by Edgar, Austol's brother-in-law. Not waiting for the maid to announce him, he burst in.

'Mistress Eliza, I think you should return to Roscarne!' He ignored Austol who had risen in protest. 'I have just returned from Penzance - Mistress Grace has been visiting Rose Quinn, but apparently she has been taken ill.'

'Who is not well? Rose or Grace?' demanded a shocked Eliza.

'Your sister! Mistress Grace! Mr. Quinn is driving her back to Roscarne and he asked me to alert you – and of course I promised to fetch you.' He stopped, out of breath.

'I shall return to Roscarne immediately,' said Eliza. 'Caroline, Tobias – come at once. Austol, please forgive us for disrupting your tea party. Another time, perhaps.'

'Of course, of course.'

'I shall accompany you,' declared Edgar. 'I may be of help. Barnabas, apparently, has gone to Falmouth and will not be back till the end of the day.' Eliza had time for the thought that her husband had wished to stay at Roscarne to work. Strange. And why had Grace called on Seth and Rose? Rose had been very impatient with Grace and her moods and tantrums in the early days and they had never been close.

Her heart jumped as she recognised Seth's carriage in the driveway of Roscarne. Edgar helped her down from the pony and trap just as Seth himself appeared at the door. Would she never be able to see him without her disobedient body fluttering like a bird caught in a net? Summoning all her strength, she greeted him coolly and waited for news of Grace.

'I am so sorry!' Seth's dark eyes gazed at her sympathetically. Perhaps there was more than sympathy there? Eliza dismissed that idea. He had left for Arizona – with Rose – had he not?

'She has a fever and has been demanding to see you. I have sent for Dr. Trevell who should be on his way as we speak.'

'She has been asking for me? For me?' Eliza could not keep the surprise from her tone. Usually Grace had very little time for her own sister, preferring to commune with Ewella or travel out to see Morwenna Tregadillett, the minister's wife. Otherwise she kept to her room, even discouraging her own children from interrupting her. As if Eliza's thoughts had summoned him, Richard came rushing out of the door, pushing Ewella aside unceremoniously.

'Aunt Eliza, Aunt Eliza, please come quickly. My mother is very ill!'

5

Grace was lying on her bed, her eyes closed and two hectic red patches on her cheeks. As Eliza entered she sat bolt upright and screamed:

'Where is James? He was here just now! I want James and nobody else! Not you, Eliza! You took Barnabas from me. Now you are trying to take James!' She lunged at Eliza, her fingers clawed as if trying to scratch her face and then she collapsed again, sobbing uncontrollably. At this point Seth appeared with Dr. Trevell to find Eliza shocked and speechless.

'Perhaps everyone should leave me with my patient,' suggested the doctor. Obediently they filed outside and gathered in the hallway.

'If you don't mind, Mistress Eliza, I should like to stay and hear the doctor's verdict,' said Seth, quietly. 'Rose is very concerned. As you know, she was close to you all when she lived here.'

'Always Rose,' thought Eliza tiredly.

'I shall stay too,' said Edgar. 'Someone should be here until Barnabas returns.'

'There is no need,' said Seth quickly. 'I shall be here. Perhaps you should get back to the Manor? I am sure Austol will want to know what is happening.' His voice was silky. Edgar frowned. The animosity between the two men still roiled under the surface but Edgar had toughened up.

'I should not be happy to leave Mistress Eliza at such a time,' he replied. 'And you, surely, will not leave your wife for long? I believe she, too, is not in the best of health?' Seth shrugged irritably.

'She knows where I am – ' he began. Eliza was just about to enter the fray when the door opened and Dr. Trevell reappeared. He looked worried, his forehead creased into even more wrinkles than before and his shaggy whiskers drooping like un-starched washing.

'Mistress Ewella – some refreshment would be more than welcome, my dear.' The endearment galvanised Ewella into rushing down to the kitchen.

'I have given Mistress Grace a sedative but I am not sure how long it will last. I need to speak to you of course, Mistress Eliza, and then Master Richard and young Elestren. Where is she at the moment?'

'She's out for her daily dose of fresh air with Nanny Hannah. She should be back soon.'

'I'll see if I can find them,' offered Edgar. Seth spoke up.

'And if it is acceptable I should like to stay. Of course, only if you agree, Mistress Eliza!' One look from those dark eyes and Eliza was lost.

'Richard. You first. Dr. Trevell's voice was grave. 'This is important and you should tell Elestren. Please do not visit your mother unless one of the family is with you. Mistress Grace is not clear in her mind and feels that everyone is opposing her and she is not averse to hitting out. You should not be alone with her.'

'She is my mother!'

'No, Richard. She is a stranger when she is like this.' Richard looked so puzzled and sad that Eliza longed to hug him. But obediently he went off to find Edgar and Elestren, his sister, while Dr. Trevell turned to Eliza and Seth.

'I can offer you little comfort. She has lost touch with reality – not for the first time, I gather, but she still has strength and can attack. I took away her scissors to be sure but you need to be careful and I hope you will impress that on Mr. Trevannion.' To Eliza's annoyance, he added. 'Perhaps you will speak to him, Mr. Quinn? Assure him there has been no exaggeration, though I am sure, Mistress Eliza, that you understand that.' She gave him a weak smile.

'She still has a fever but I could not get near her to examine her further. I shall return tomorrow after I have consulted with a fellow doctor. This is an unusual case when someone such as Grace turns against her whole family and she only feels safe with an outsider. It is possible that we may have to move her to a hospital or clinic – '

'NO!' said Eliza. 'We shall find a way to help her.'

When Dr. Trevell had gone, after partaking of the refreshments Ewella provided, Eliza and Seth were left alone in the drawing room.

'This must be a dreadful shock for you,' ventured Seth.

'I have had a few shocks in my life,' Eliza said and was gratified to see Seth colour. He did not pretend to misunderstand her.

'Eliza – there was nothing else I could do!' he burst out.' I explained it all to you before. I was desperate to remain near you but I knew that I could hope for nothing more. There was Barnabas after all. And in a moment of misjudgement I thought the solution was to marry Rose. That would have been my entry into your family. Please do not misunderstand me – I am very fond of Rose. She is a lovely and sensible woman but I used her to stay near to you. And I was ashamed that I did that. So I felt we should all have a better chance if Rose and I moved to Arizona, where at least I had the mine.'

'You and Barnabas both left me.' Eliza's voice shook.

'Oh, Eliza!' Seth leaned forward in his chair and took her hands in his. 'I had no idea that Barnabas would be away so long! Or that he had consigned you to such a house as Carnglaze!'

Eliza remained still. Her hands, lost in Seth's, made her so aware of him that she wanted to cling to him, to feel his arms around her and more. Just as before, his mere presence close to her made her feel out of control, ready to sacrifice everything she valued to be with him. The abrupt entry of Richard saved her. His distress showed clearly on his face. Hardly glancing at Seth he looked pleadingly at Eliza.

'Please come with me to see my mother! Ewella said she is asleep so there is no point. But I do want to see her. I should be near her when she is so ill.'

'I shall come with you,' said Seth. 'If she is asleep, perhaps you can sit next to her for a while. That will comfort you – and probably she will feel better for your presence.'

'I don't think she really cares if I am near her or not,' said Richard, without any self-pity. 'But I shall feel better.'

For an hour, Richard sat close by the bed and Eliza and Seth sat on the chaise longue by the window. Grace lay, her eyes closed, her lashes sweeping her cheeks and the hectic red flushes gone. She looked very beautiful, her stillness contrasting with the vicious temper she had displayed earlier. Earnestly, Eliza hoped that she would come back to a realisation of where she was and who she was. This was her sister after all. Though their relationship had been scarred by jealousy and animosity, she had begun to hope that as they grew older they would become closer. That meant, of course, she would have to forget her own helpless rage at Barnabas' infidelity and the part that Grace had played and forgive the hurtful gossip that had dogged her for so long. Deep in her thoughts, she missed the slight stirring of her sister.

Seth, however, had not. He motioned Richard away from his mother's side and he moved closer to check her mood if she woke. When she did it was to baffle him entirely.

'Oh James! It IS you. You have come back to me. I have been waiting so long.' With a beatific smile on her face she grasped Seth's hand.

'Please sit with me. I do not like being alone. I always seem to be alone. All my life I have been alone. But then you came along……..' her voice tailed away.

Seth sat down beside her while Eliza and Richard watched helplessly. Grace, a look of contentment on her face, finally drifted back to sleep. Eliza felt herself torn by conflicting emotions. Sorrow for Grace, who was clearly still confused. Then a deep regret that she, Eliza, had not recognised the essential loneliness of her sister right from childhood. Tears welled up as the enormity of that statement 'I always seem to be alone' broke over her like a storm wave. How could she not have realised how her sister had always felt? She remembered how Grace had resented her friendship with Rose in their younger days and how she had tagged along, a poor third in their trio; then there was her sad, unrequited love for Barnabas, followed by the loss of her husband, James Treloyhan. And her desperation for a child – not for herself but to please James. How unhappy she must have been so many times in her life.

'She must not be left alone!' said Eliza, fiercely. 'There must be someone with her at all times. I cannot bear to think of her waking up to an empty room.'

'The children should not be with her on their own – Dr. Trevell was adamant about that.' said Seth. Eliza nodded.

'We must apportion time as best we can. I shall do the first stint and perhaps you, Seth, could talk to Edgar and Ewella'

'I think Kenwyn would come over and help. At least Grace knows him.' said Seth. 'I think it would be even more frightening for her if she woke to a stranger in her room. Allow me a moment to send a message back to Rose with my driver and I shall be here until Dr. Trevell decides what must be done.' For once, Seth's obvious concern for Rose did not upset Eliza. She was determined to focus on her sister and do what she could to help her.

Eliza sat with Grace all that night, a single candle flickering on the little table. The sedative at last seemed to have taken hold and Grace slept peacefully. Seth tiptoed in to relieve Eliza but she waved him away.

'I shall be here till morning,' she insisted. 'Then you can take over.' Rather doubtfully, Seth nodded and left Eliza curled in an armchair. But the stresses of the previous days were too much for her. Gradually her eyes closed and for the greater part of the night the two sisters slept, as they had done as children, separately and yet together.

The dawn light woke Eliza. The pain in her limbs from her contorted position in the armchair made her groan. Carefully she unknotted herself and stood up, stretching. Then she looked over to Grace's bed. It was empty.

6

The house was still. It was too early for anyone to be stirring so a panicky Eliza decided to start searching on her own. Closed doors, empty corridors, and no sign of her errant sister in the house. Try the garden – which she did. No luck. With sinking heart, Eliza realised that she had one option left. She would have to search the rocks and caves along the shore – not an easy task. Resolutely she began the scramble down to the shore line, praying that Grace would have come to no harm. The pearl coloured sea was reassuringly calm, and sand and sky stretched away into the distance in muted shades of grey, peaceful and un-alarming. The rocks of Marah Cove were partially covered by the incoming tide which was advancing in slow and nonchalant manner, deceptive to strangers. A strong smell of seaweed pervaded the air and the gulls were swooping and diving as usual, calling and crying to each other.

Of Grace there was no sign. Where could her sister be? She had searched the caves in the vicinity, calling for Grace, her voice echoing in the empty spaces. No answers and no Grace. There was only one thing she could do. She would have to return to Roscarne and admit that she had let her sister escape during the night. Seth would be so disappointed in her. Ewella would take the opportunity to declare that Grace was such trouble because she was spoilt. Nanny Hannah would click her tongue and scurry off to tend to Elestren, her disapproval trailing after her like the tail of a comet. And Richard? The thought of letting Richard down was worst of all. What about Barnabas? He would be scathing but she had not thought of him at all. He never seemed to be around when needed.

In the kitchen, Mrs. Adwyn was busy with baking and she looked up in surprise when Eliza entered.

'Mistress Eliza! They 'ave all been looking for you!' she exclaimed'

'Looking for ME?'

'Mistress Grace was fair upset when she woke and you were not there. I believe Mr. Quinn has been taking care of her.' Eliza shook her head in bewilderment.

'What about Mr. Barnabas?'

'He came in very late from Falmouth, so Ewella said, and did not want to be woke up for breakfast.' Curiosity sharpened her tone. Why did her mistress not know where her husband was?

'Thank you Mrs. Adwyn,' said Eliza, with dignity. She would find out for herself what was happening.

'Mistress Eliza!' It was Ewella.

'What is going on! How long since Grace returned?'

'I did not know she had been anywhere. But mark my words, she has been mischief making. I know her expressions. Just now she looks like a pilchard that swallowed a shark.'

'Oh, Ewella, give her some leeway. She has not been well, you know.' Ewella shrugged her shoulders. That excuse had been used too often.

'You'll see. She is in the rhododendron garden with Mr. Quinn.'

'And the children?'

'Waiting for Miss Maisie in the school room.'

Eliza hurried into the rhododendron garden at the front of the house. The sun had risen, like a shiny new penny, and the moors were vibrant with colour. The sound of Grace's laughter drifted to her; then she saw them. Grace, dressed in lilac silk, her blonde hair loose over her shoulders, was hanging on to Seth's arm and laughing up at him as if she had not a care in the world. To be fair, Seth did look a little strained, and when he caught sight of Eliza, somewhat more than that. Grace's voice contained unmistakeable triumph.

'This is dear Seth who will look after me until James returns. That may be a long time of course – but I shall not worry. I feel safe with Seth. He is a real friend – a true friend.' Seth looked as if he wished the ground would swallow him and Eliza had to choke on the chuckle that rose in her throat. It was rare indeed to see him discomfited.

'How kind of you, Mr. Quinn,' she said. 'But perhaps, Grace, you should come in now and rest.' At this, her sister shot her a look of such venom that she was taken aback.

'I do not wish to come in,' said Grace. 'You just want to take Seth away. Like you always take away what is mine.' She had reverted to a sulky child.

'That is not true!' said Eliza, stung. Her impulse to laugh vanished. Ewella was right. Grace was bent on mischief making, lost in her shadowed, disordered world. And there was nothing that she, Eliza, could do to change that.

'We shall go in, now,' said Seth, soothingly. 'Perhaps a drink and some saffron cake would be attractive?' Grace pouted, considering the offer.

'Only if you stay with me,' she said at last. 'And not with you, Eliza.' She spat the words at her sister, the enmity spilling out into the open and Eliza, unwillingly and finally, had to recognise that Grace did not regard her as a friend. Her dislike for her elder sister had risen to the surface like foam on the sea. Seth looked alarmed and hastened to act as peacemaker

'I am sure Mistress Eliza will not object to my accompanying you to take some refreshment,' he said. 'I am partial to saffron cake myself.'

Quite put out, Eliza decided to visit Uncle Tobias, now safely ensconced in his new study, a considerably larger room than he had occupied previously. His favourite armchair took pride of place by the window and his precious mining books at last had place in a mahogany bookcase. Dark green velvet curtains guarded his privacy when he wanted to nap during the day and the carpet, he said, was warmer and softer than the fleece from a sheep.

'Eliza, I have to keep pinching myself that we have actually left Carnglaze and its discomforts behind us,' he said with a welcoming smile. Eliza was glad to see that he looked much fitter than before, his eyes brighter and the bronchial choke absent from his voice.

'I declare, Uncle, you look years younger,' his niece laughed and Tobias smiled at the compliment. Then he frowned.

'I cannot say the same for you, my dear,' he said. 'You look burdened by cares.'

'Grace.' said Eliza, briefly.' I have been searching for her along the shore and somehow she gave me the slip and I found her in the gardens with Seth. And she hates me. I know she does.' The sad admission left her lips without volition

'Eliza, I think a nip of my best brandy is called for,' said her uncle. 'In that cupboard there.'

'Uncle, are you feeling ill?' Eliza was immediately worried.

'No! YOU need the brandy and I will join you.' They laughed together and Eliza felt that the world was not such a bleak place after all.

'You have to remember, Eliza, that Grace has always been wilful and a rival to you. The illness she has makes it impossible to hide what she feels and possibly exaggerates those same feelings. Take no heed. She will swing round like a weathercock and remember that you are her only sister and that you care for her. Perhaps you should confide more in Barnabas – that husband of yours spends too much time with his consortium and his mines. He should be more help to you.'

'He is so busy,' sighed Eliza. 'But thank you, Uncle, I feel much better – and I am getting a taste for brandy!'

'Good. Then you will visit me more often.'

'Mama!' Caroline was curled up in a chair in the drawing room.

'Caroline, my dear. Why are you so pale just now? Is anything wrong?'

'No – er, yes. No, that is….'

'Try again. Start at the beginning,' smiled her mother.

'I have been dreaming – and the dreams seem to cast a shadow over my day and they worry me – and they keep coming back as if they are trying to tell me something – '

'What were you dreaming about?'

'Water – too much water – and storm clouds hiding the sun - just like I dreamed at Carnglaze. Always clouds drifting over the sun. And – I feel we are threatened.' And Caroline burst into tears. Eliza put an arm around her shoulders.

'My dear – they are just dreams…' she began.

'Yes, just like Jael had sometimes. And you know Mistress Annie said I, too, had the sight.'

Eliza could not deny this was true. She remembered how Caroline had dreamed of water just before the mines were flooded. She had had premonitions as had Jael. Now what could happen?

Before she could follow that train of thought any further, the sound of raised voices interrupted her. Grace was screaming at the top of her voice, the gist being that everyone had deserted her. Seth could be heard trying to calm her and comfort her, assuring her that he would be back soon.

'What on earth is wrong?' Barnabas had evidently returned. Eliza entered the hallway just in time to see Grace rushing up the stairs in a tantrum.

'I have to go back to Rose,' said Seth, worriedly. 'I cannot leave her alone any longer. I tried to assure Grace that I would be back but she was not in a mood to listen.'

'I'm afraid she latches on to one individual and expects to receive total attention,' said Barnabas in exasperated tone. 'It is her illness makes her so unreasonable. Eliza, my dear, perhaps it is time for your sister to be given her sedative?'

'No,' said Eliza decidedly. 'Dr. Trevell said once a day. And she has had her dose for today.'

'Surely – when it is obviously needed?'

'I would not care to go against the doctor's advice.' Eliza faced up to her husband whose blue eyes were flashing – more in annoyance at Eliza's defiance than her sister's behaviour. Seth murmured awkwardly that he should leave but Barnabas put his hand out to stop him.

'I am so sorry, Seth, that Grace should have cornered you in such a way and we both – fixing Eliza with a steely stare – owe you our gratitude for being so patient with her. She will soon turn her attention to someone else. However I do recognise how worrying it must be to leave Rose – '

'She is not well at the moment,' said Seth 'and inclined to depression. Even though she has been spending her time with the ladies' sewing circle and enjoying the chatter, I feel I should be with her more often.' His words fell like stones on poor Eliza. She was hated by her sister. Her husband was angry with her because of the disruption caused by her sister's presence – and now Seth was declaring that Rose needed him and that he would have to leave Roscarne. Quite rightly so, Eliza allowed. Rose was his wife and she, Eliza, had no claims on Seth. Except that she loved him and she knew that he loved her.

Ewella came bustling in to announce that lunch would be ready soon and, of course, to find out what was going on.

'I am so sorry, Mistress Ewella. I was just leaving,' said Seth. 'I shall not be able to stay to lunch. Rose wishes to be remembered to you. She misses seeing you all more often, but her health does not allow for too much travelling.'

'That's it!' Barnabas exclaimed, smiting his forehead. 'I have the perfect solution! I do not know why I did not think of it before! Perhaps you would consider coming to live here with Rose? Think of it. You and Rose living at Roscarne! I need you, as a member of the consortium, to confer with, and Rose would be a delightful companion for Eliza. They were always good friends! That would put an end to all this backwards and forwards for you and bring great advantages to us! You did say that your house hunting has not been successful.'

Seth, put on the spot, did not know what to say. The colour drained from Eliza's face. Seth – and Rose – in the same house? How could she bear it? Her shock was aggravated by anger. Surely Barnabas should have discussed such an invitation with her before announcing it? Ewella watched the interplay between the three of them with interest. It was a good idea. Why was Eliza so obviously disconcerted? This would bear watching. For her part she felt it would be good to have another man in the house. Barnabas was so often absent for long periods during the day and sometimes for several days at a time. If Mistress Grace became out of control – or Uncle Tobias fell ill – or any other eventuality – it would be a boon to have Seth around. Of course he also would be out for much of the time - her musing was interrupted by Seth leaving, promising that he would talk to Rose. He avoided Eliza's eyes, the pleading in them. But what did she want? She did not know herself.

7

'Are you sure this is a good idea?' Eliza ventured. 'I know we have the room but perhaps .....
'I thought it was a touch of inspiration,' said Barnabas who seemed in a high good mood. 'Why? What have you against the idea? I thought you would be delighted to have Rose at Roscarne again?'
'Yes, but I'm not sure how Grace will receive the news.' Eliza knew she was prevaricating but could not help herself. The prospect of being so near Seth for much of the time had thrown her into disarray.
'Take no heed of Grace!' Barnabas dismissed his sister-in-law with an airy wave of the hand. 'She has to learn that she cannot have everything her own way.'
'But she has never had things her own way – that is why she has been so unhappy,' persisted Eliza. 'I realise now that so much of her apparent selfishness is because she feels she has to fight for what she wants – and all that started when Rose and I were friends and she felt left out. And then when you and I were married....'
'Enough of that!' snapped Barnabas, his good mood evaporating. 'She has been a thorn in my side for too long and caused me considerable grief –'
'Caused YOU considerable grief?' Eliza could not believe her ears. 'I believe it is fair to say that the 'grief' as you call it was mine.'
'Yes, well,' said Barnabas gruffly. 'There is no point in raking all that up again. I shall invite Rose and Seth to stay at Roscarne for as long as they wish and there's an end to it.'
'But – '

'Dammit, Eliza!' Barnabas thumped the table with his fist. 'Enough!' Eliza looked coolly at her irate husband. His decision, not hers. Her back iron straight, she stalked from the room.

'My brother in a temper again?' probed Ewella. Eliza shrugged her shoulders.

'I think mining problems are weighing on him. At this rate we shall be back at Carnglaze while he travels to Timbuctoo or anywhere else he can find far away!' She marched off to see how Miss Maisie was faring in the schoolroom.

She found Caroline, Nessa and Richard, heads bent over their books and Elestren drawing busily on her slate. Of Joel there was no sign. Miss Maisie, her hair on end as if combed by a high wind, a sure sign of discipline distress, was writing questions on the blackboard.

'I do not know where Joel has gone!' she said. 'I turned round and he was not there. It is not the first time he has missed lessons. I think the time has come to report him to Mr. Barnabas.'

'Perhaps I can find out what he is up to,' said Eliza, soothingly. 'I am so sorry that he is giving you such trouble, Miss Maisie, but I think it is inadvisable to alert Mr. Barnabas just now. He has business worries and is not in the best of moods.' She was not going to admit that, yet again, her opposition to her husband's suggestions had been instrumental in rousing his ire. Miss Maisie nodded, glad that she would not have to face the master of the house and his uncertain temper herself. Caroline and Nessa did not look up from their work, but Richard looked as if he were about to protest.

'Richard, please come with me for a moment,' said Eliza.

'Did you want to say something?' she asked, once outside the door. Richard looked uncomfortable but Eliza was struck anew by his steady grey eyes. What a handsome boy he was. And how carelessly his mother treated him. Not for the first time, she wished that he was a member of her brood and that she could make up for Grace's shortcomings.

'Come with me to the kitchen,' she decided. 'We shall see if Mrs. Adwyn has made any more of those ginger biscuits.'

Finally, over milk and ginger biscuits, Richard was able to confide that Joel did not like lessons because he felt unable to do them and was miserable as a result.

'But Richard – Joel always seems to be joking and laughing. Surely he can't be miserable as you say?'

'He does that to hide what he is really feeling,' said Richard earnestly. 'He was very upset when Miss Maisie said he was working too slowly. There were tears in his eyes and he did not want anyone to see so he slipped out when her back was turned.'

'Oh Richard!' That a boy of ten years old could see so clearly what was wrong made her feel negligent. As a mother, she should have realised what was going on much earlier.

'Richard – I am beholden to you. Thank you for pointing out what happened. I shall do what I can to remedy the situation.' Richard smiled gratefully and made his escape back to the schoolroom.

'I should now consult Barnabas,' thought Eliza. Then decided against it. One clash per day was enough. Besides, she knew what she wanted to do. She would take Joel on his own for some of his lessons and see if she could help him. She broached this idea to Miss Maisie who fell on it like a mouse offered cheese.

'It would help so much,' she said fervently.' I spend more time with him than the others and that is not fair. I shall show you what we are doing and you can follow that if you wish – or you may want to make up your own timetable?'

Joel seemed pleasantly surprised that his mother was going to take a hand in his education. Not so Barnabas.

'Why was I not informed of this?' he demanded, in a dangerously quiet voice, finding Eliza and Joel working on numbers together.

'You seem to be rather busy just now,' replied Eliza, sweetly. 'Joel and I are just going over his tables.'

'Why not with Miss Maisie?'

'Why not with me?' Eliza rapped back. 'He is my child and I have the time to give him some attention!'

'Come Eliza, be reasonable. You are not a governess in this house. Miss Maisie holds that position – '

'Yes, but ....'

'No buts. You are my wife and have other responsibilities – and I am paying Miss Maisie for what she is apparently not doing.'

'Joel, please wait for me in the kitchen. Ask Mrs. Adwyn for milk and a ginger biscuit. I shall not be long but I wish to talk to your father.' Joel looked from one to the other, big eyed and then scuttled off.

'Joel has been difficult of late,' said Eliza. 'And I have been helping out. It has not been a problem for me and as far as I am aware, I have not failed to undertake my other 'responsibilities' whatever they may be.'

'Eliza, you insisted that Joel should not go to school and this is what happens. He needs discipline as I have said to you before.'

'Discipline is the last thing he needs,' Eliza protested and told Barnabas what Richard had said. Barnabas listened but looked unconvinced.

'He is my son. You only have to look at the colour of his hair! I refuse to believe that he is slow – or that he misbehaves in order to cover up that fact.'

'What do you want me to do, then?' Eliza made her voice as placatory as she could. If she antagonized her husband further, she knew that he would pack Joel off to school and she would be unable to stop him. Barnabas looked surprised at this sudden climb down.

'We shall wait until the beginning of the new term and then decide. Meanwhile you should take the time to organise the east wing for the arrival of the Quinns. They will move in at the end of the week.'

Barnabas strode off, leaving Eliza gasping at the sudden blow. Of course it would be lovely to have Rose so near at hand – but Seth? Even though Barnabas would monopolise much of his time, there would be endless moments when they would not be able to avoid seeing each other; there would be unexpected meetings – she shivered at the thought. But the excitement inside her, the faster beating of her heart she could not obliterate. Seth would be staying in Roscarne and she, Eliza, was glad of it.

8

Barnabas made sure he was there to welcome Seth and Rose when they arrived. It was a cool day, warning of the winter to come, and Rose was wrapped in a luxurious fur cape into which she nestled, looking out wide eyed as if she could not believe she was actually there at Roscarne. So Seth was taking great care of his wife, Eliza noted. He was ensuring that she had the best, from the fur cape to the green velvet gown she wore and her collared necklace, a new fashion, sparkled with what could be diamonds. But Rose herself. Eliza caught her breath. She was sallow, her skin tired, her eyes circled with dark shadows and her hair, just visible under her toque, seemed without life. Eliza stepped forward, all hesitations forgotten. This was Rose, her friend of so many years, Rose whose unhappiness had left its mark for everyone to see.

'Rose! Welcome to Roscarne again! We are so pleased to have you here!' The warmth of her greeting made Barnabas smile in approval and Seth heave a sigh of relief

'I can't believe it!' Rose cried. 'We have been looking for a house but nothing we have seen compares to Roscarne. And here we are! And we shall be together as before!' Arms around each other, the two women, girls no longer, made their way to the east wing where a maid was already busy unpacking.

Rose and Seth were absorbed into the life of Roscarne as if they had always been there. Barnabas derived new energy from Seth and his companionship and the two schemed happily to open another mine. 'An experimental mine,' Barnabas confided enthusiastically to Eliza, 'Where we can try out different ways of tunnelling, different materials to support the walls, different ways of extracting ore at the deeper levels – and, of course, new methods of pumping to extend the depths we can reach.' He paused for breath and Eliza smiled, delighted with his new attitude and particularly with his desire to confront those more conservative in their ideas, elderly men, heavily whiskered and pawky in their stiff white collars, unwilling to risk their money on radical proposals. However, Seth provided considerable investment which dowsed any complaints about more innovations, particularly if they were confined to the new mine. Uncle Tobias entered into the discussions and debates with verve and Eliza saw that he, too, had a new interest in his life.

Meanwhile, she and Rose could not stop talking, catching up without awkwardness on the years they had missed.

'It seems that we have been apart for a lifetime,' exclaimed Rose. 'There seems to be so much to say and we have had such different experiences!' And she went on to describe life in Arizona – the vastness and the beauty of the Mojave desert, the sadness of wandering, displaced Indians, the spread of Indian reserves, and the growing townships in the midst of miles of nothing. She talked of the strange feeling of isolation she experienced when she stood at her door and realised the landscape before her was empty, entirely empty and that she was alone until Seth returned.

'I could watch the setting sun turn the mountains to blue and purple; I could see an occasional eagle swooping low and it was really beautiful but as the night approached I felt the darkness was like a thick forest around us and we were cut off from everything.'

'But did you not have servants? Surely you had a maid?' Eliza was surprised.

'We were living in a shack!' said Rose. 'I knew it was only temporary and Seth did all that was needed when I was ill. At last we had company when he hired miners for his gold mine which he was reopening. But only one of them brought his wife and she and I did not become friends....'

Eliza realised that perhaps Rose's life had not been as idyllic as she had imagined.

'So you see, I was delighted to return to Cornwall – and to you and your family.'

Then she demanded to know what had happened at Carnglaze. – 'Were you really haunted? Did you actually see a ghost?' and it was Eliza's turn to describe a life that had fast receded into the past, a life that she could hardly believe in herself.

'You would not believe the state of the house when we arrived! It was dirty and decrepit but that was not the worst – it had an atmosphere, a strange atmosphere and eventually I realised that we were being haunted. There was one voice that kept sobbing and then another one - or it might have been the same one - singing nursery rhymes. Then it went from bad to worse.'

'Worse?' shivered Rose. 'I would have been terrified!'

'We heard the jingle of harnesses as if there were many ponies outside and the voices of men but when we looked out there was nothing there.'

'What did the children think about it all?'

'Caroline was the one it affected most. You remember how sensitive she was – she still is.'

Seth spent most of his time closeted with Barnabas in his study when home and, it seemed to Eliza, that he made elaborate manoeuvres to avoid being left alone with her. One such time she entered the drawing room and he was reading in an armchair. He jumped to his feet, ready to flee.

'The door is over there,' said Eliza, pushed to sarcasm. 'If you are quick I won't even see you and you can pretend you have not seen me.'

Seth hesitated, clearly at a loss, then he sighed heavily. At last he made up his mind. He spoke slowly.

'Eliza – I see you. Make no mistake. I see you. I know where you are in the house, I see you in the gardens. I feel bereft when you go out, then I feel I am leaving you behind when I go to the mines. But at least I know I shall see you at mealtimes and when I go to sleep I know we are under the same roof and it gives me comfort. I wake in the morning with renewed energy because I know you will be there.'

Eliza could not believe what she was hearing. Seth, usually so confident, so self-assured, so adept at avoiding her company, admitting that he did think of her, that he did want to be near her …

'I – I thought you were determined to forget any bond between us,' she murmured.

'I thought it wise to do so,' he began. 'But like all untruths, based on self-deception, I find it impossible. Eliza, I have never forgotten what has passed between us. You are the light in the house for me but I have to hide that from everyone else.'

Eliza looked up at him, the colour mounting to her face, her eyes bright.

'Seth, just knowing how you feel has made such a difference to me,' she whispered. Then paused. 'I do not want to take you away from Rose, please believe me. I know that you are honourable and would never leave her. And Barnabas is my husband and I have children – but surely, surely I am allowed my private feelings as you are.' Impulsively she moved towards him and found herself where she had wanted to be – clasped in his arms. Then he pushed her gently away.

'We must take care. Know, Eliza, that I love you and have for a very long time. I do not know what will happen in the future but for now, I am happy just to be near you.'

'And I you,' she said breathlessly. The words seem to take shape and hover above them as if the air in the drawing room bore witness to their confessed feelings. They were interrupted by Ewella. She looked from one to the other, puzzled by the tension, then announced that Sir Austol Treloyhan was waiting to see Mistress Eliza.

'Show him in here,' said Seth. 'I was just leaving.'

Eliza could have wished Austol to be anywhere else but she pasted a smile on her face to greet him, wondering what he wanted this time. Austol wasted no moments in greeting, his words pouring out with an urgency unusual for him.

'I am having further trouble with Lamorna. She is fixated on the idea of going to an Art school in London. You are aware of that. But I have another piece of news that should interest you. She and Nathaniel have been writing to each other! And apparently he has been encouraging her!'

'I had no idea that they were in touch!' exclaimed Eliza. 'But surely writing letters should do no harm? I am glad that he is writing to someone as he hardly communicates with us during term time.'

'I am NOT pleased! Lamorna is only fourteen and she does not need a sixteen year old boy giving her advice!' Eliza sighed.

'Nathaniel and John will be home for the holidays in a few weeks so perhaps I can talk to him then. Otherwise I am not sure what I can do.'

'I need to talk to Barnabas,' said Austol, irritably. 'This cannot go on! Lamorna is becoming more defiant and it is affecting the rest of my girls. Surely, Eliza, you can see my difficulty?'

'What I see,' said Eliza carefully, 'Is a daughter who has inherited an interest in art that is shared by her father. Moreover she has a talent for painting and wishes to develop it by attending Art school. That I understand. But of course, defying you is another matter.'

'You think I am being unreasonable?'

'No, no. But I think you need to avoid taking up an entrenched position that prevents you discussing matters with her. The days are past when parents can demand unquestioning obedience from their children.'

'I do not believe that! Maybe that happens in some families. But Lamorna is of an age when she should obey me without question. I am sure Barnabas would expect nothing less – especially from a girl.' Austol fixed a basilisk stare on Eliza.

'What would you do? Tell me.'

'Austol – you are putting me in an impossible position! I cannot advise you on a course of action! She is your daughter. And you and I have different views on the desirability of total obedience. I think you risk losing her altogether when she is a year or two older if you persist in demanding that from her.'

Before Austol could say anything more, the door opened and in floated Grace. She was dressed in lavender chiffon which swirled about her and a cap of lace so fine it must have come from France.

'Oh, Austol, how delightful to see you,' she cooed, to Austol's astonishment and Eliza's relief. A hostile Grace would have been the last straw. She held out her hands to Austol and said confidentially: 'Of course you know that James is back? We have had such a pleasant time walking in the garden.'

'No. Grace, you were walking in the garden with Mr. Quinn!' said Eliza firmly. It was time her sister was cured of that particular delusion. Grace pouted.

'I know YOU do not care for James and I to be back together. Perhaps it would be a good idea if you moved away and then you cannot be always casting doubt on what is happening! Especially when it is something good for me!' Eliza could see that Grace was working herself up into a tantrum. As if in answer to her unspoken plea, Ewella appeared and ushered Grace out of the room with the promise of herbal tea and freshly baked ginger cake.

'I see, Mistress Eliza, that you have your own problems,' said Austol, stiffly. 'Mistress Grace does not seem to have improved.'

'No. Her periods of lucidity are shorter and sometimes a whole day will pass and she will still be in a world of her own. But' – she forestalled Austol's next

comment – 'she also has days of sweet temper and contentment and during these times she is no trouble at all.'
Austol looked unconvinced but at least Grace had diverted him from the problem of Lamorna.

'Please come and see Uncle Tobias. He does so welcome company,' said Eliza persuasively.

'I did not know how to answer him,' she confided to Rose, later. 'And I am not sure I should tell Barnabas about Nathaniel either. I feel he would not approve.'

'Of course you should tell Barnabas! He is Nathaniel's father!' Rose was shocked. This gave Eliza pause for thought.

'I suppose you are right,' she admitted. 'I was just hoping to avoid another confrontation with my husband. I do so value you being here, Rose, and I know your advice is always wise.'
Rose flushed with pleasure.

'I can only say what I think,' she said. 'But of course it is you who has to face Barnabas.'

His reaction was as his wife predicted.

'That boy should be attending to his schoolwork – not fomenting rebellion in Austol's daughter!' he snapped. 'I shall write to him!'

'Do you think that he will take notice?' asked Eliza. 'Nathaniel was already determined to follow his own path when he left Roscarne for school.'

'He will do as I say!'

'I wonder how Caroline will feel?' mused Eliza, unwilling to argue further. 'She misses him dreadfully – and when he comes home at the end of term she will expect him to be a companion as before.'

'I expect Austol will take care to keep Lamorna out of harm's way.' said Barnabas. 'And I shall have a word with my son!'

9

Barnabas contrived to cause further upset just as the household at Roscarne was beginning to settle down. He announced that he would be going to London for a few days, calling in at Exeter to see Nathaniel. A faint touch of defiance in his voice suggested he knew it would be an unpopular decision.

'How long exactly do you mean by a few days?' asked Eliza, innocently. 'Last time you went away you did not come back for two years!'

Barnabas laughed. He was looking very relaxed and prosperous, lounging in an armchair, provoking in his wife an irrational desire to slap him. So she was to be left to deal with an irate Austol, a difficult Grace and Ewella, always so uncertain in her moods. Then there was Joel. She dared not think about Seth and Rose.

'Probably a week – two weeks. I really do not know,' said Barnabas easily. 'I have hopes of gaining new investment for our latest experimental mine. Also, as you might have guessed, I intend to call in on Nathaniel. I need to nip his little romance in the bud.'

'Oh, Barnabas! We do not know if it is a romance,' said Eliza. 'You may make things worse. You know how independent Nathaniel is.' She realised, too late, that she had said exactly the wrong thing to her husband.

'I think I know how to deal with my own son,' he said, his words clipped and cold.

'Of course,' said Eliza, hurriedly. But his good mood had gone and he strode out of the drawing room.

'I was really tactless, Rose. I should know better by now. But he does not believe in discussion any more. After all, Nathaniel is my son, too.'

'And you are lucky to have him,' replied Rose and again Eliza knew she had been careless with the feelings of others.

It was Uncle Tobias who came to her defence.

'He has responsibilities here in Roscarne,' he croaked. 'The mines are important but they are secondary to the well-being of his family. And as for Nathaniel, he will trample over that boy like a bull elephant and it will do no good.'

'That is exactly what worries me,' sighed Eliza.

'Don't you upset yourself, my dear, you still have Seth here and he seems to be sensible. I am not surprised that Barnabas relies on him. How is Rose, just now? I thought she was looking a little brighter just recently.'

'I think being back at Roscarne is suiting her,' agreed Eliza.

Indeed, Rose appeared happier, more ready to smile and there was more colour in her cheeks. Seth was less inclined to hover round her, looking anxious. He was a success with Ewella and Mrs. Adwyn, both of whom were susceptible to an adroit compliment as well as admiring his dark good looks. He reduced Miss Maisie to self-conscious giggles, which precluded any conversation, but spurred her on to teach with more zest. It was only Eliza who found that it was necessary to avoid him to help maintain her peace of mind.

The absence of Barnabas, Eliza found, lightened the atmosphere of Roscarne. The children were less constrained at the shared mealtimes and there were fewer 'disciplinary' confrontations. She herself found that she could fall asleep straight away, undisturbed by Barnabas' erratic bedtimes and could spread herself luxuriously in the extra space. She made sure that she spent part of each day with Rose and some time with Uncle Tobias, knowing that Ewella was in her element, organising the household. Grace appeared at odd times, sometimes smiling, sometimes sullen, sometimes fussing over Richard and Elestren, more often ignoring them. Elestren was hardened to her mother's moods but Eliza could see that Richard took them to heart and she did her best to distract him and give him the attention he so obviously needed. And Seth? He watched Eliza moving around the house; he waited for her trim figure to appear on the stairs, in the morning room, in the garden; each time he saw her he felt a mixture of pleasure and frustration. She always greeted him warmly on his return from the mines and chatted cordially at mealtimes but she had put up a barrier between them, a barrier that Rose recognised with some puzzlement.

'Have you offended Eliza in some way?' she asked Seth.

'No, of course not.'

'It's just that she seems a little distant somehow and it is not like her to indulge in such lightweight conversation all the time.'

'You had better ask her!' said Seth, shortly. He knew perfectly well what Eliza was up to and while he respected her motives, he found it annoying to be kept at arms-length in such a way.

Then Austol came to call and he and Eliza were closeted in the morning room for some time. An irritated Seth left for Wheal Eliza and returned to find that she had accompanied Austol back to the Manor.

'I do not know why,' said Rose, surprised that Seth was so disturbed by the fact. 'She often goes to the Manor. It seems that Austol tends to rely on her advice when he has problems with his daughters – and with Kenwyn, of course.'

'Austol needs to find himself another wife,' said Seth, between his teeth.

'I think this is all to do with Nathaniel writing to Lamorna,' said Rose. 'No doubt Barnabas has intervened – he said he was going to call in at Exeter and if I'm any judge he will have upset everyone.'

'He has a right. He is Nathaniel's father after all.'

'I hope you would not be so autocratic with any children we may have,' said Rose bravely. Seth looked at her in astonishment. Surely she could not believe that it was possible for them still to have children?

'Rose, my dear, my concern is for you and I believe that we would settle any problems with our children together,' he smiled and Rose, comforted, smiled back.

It was late when Eliza returned with Austol's driver. She found Seth in the drawing room, clearly waiting for her return.

'Is Austol not able to manage on his own?' he queried, frowning.

'It's Lamorna. Apparently Nathaniel has been forbidden to write to her and she is beside herself, threatening to run away to London or to Exeter and Austol does not know how to deal with her. So he came to me.'

'And were you able to 'deal with her'?' asked Seth, his voice dangerously soft.

'Yes – no. Not really. But Austol has locked her in her room which will not do any good. He cannot keep her there indefinitely and she will get more defiant by the minute.'

'I think you should let Austol and Lamorna work it out on their own,' said Seth. He was unable to keep the anger out of his tone.

'Why, Seth, I think that is my decision!' Eliza replied firmly.

'No. Barnabas asked me to watch over you – '

'Rather like a fox being asked to take care of a chicken,' taunted Eliza.' I do not need to be watched over by you or Ewella or anybody else.' She turned to go, but he was beside her, blocking her access to the door. He realised that perhaps he had not been explicit enough.

'I do not trust Austol. You should not sully your good name by running to the Manor all the time to help someone who is perfectly able to help himself.'

Rigid with sudden rage Eliza tried to push past him but found herself imprisoned in his arms. All the fight went out of her and she leant against him with a sigh. She tried to say something but it was too late. For the first time he kissed her. Really kissed her. And she did nothing to stop him.

'Ah, Eliza, I want only the best for you,' he murmured, stroking her hair.

'I have been trying to avoid just this kind of temptation,' she said, helplessly. 'Let me go, Seth, or we shall be unable to stay in this house together – and yet it would be unbearable if we could not see each other at all.'

'It would be unthinkable,' agreed Seth. 'I am sorry. I forgot Rose – and Barnabas – for the moment.'

They stared at each other, unable to move away. Then abruptly, Seth turned to leave.

'I must go and find Rose,' he said. 'This was all my fault – but I do not trust Austol as I said before. He seems to have some sort of an obsession about you – '

'I think that is an exaggeration,' protested Eliza. 'He is lonely since he lost Eulalia and does not know how to manage either his household or his children.'

'Then he needs to find someone else to help him.'

'He has. Me.'

Seth was forced to laugh. 'It is no joke. I shall not make the mistake of forbidding you to go to the Manor. Barnabas can do that when he comes back.' Before Eliza could make an indignant reply he was gone.

10

'Mama – may I speak with you, please?'

'Of course, Caroline. But why so formal?'

'I want to talk to you about something important – and I do not want anybody else to know. Particularly not Father – or Ewella – or – anybody!'

'I shall respect your confidence, Caroline, of course.' Eliza hid a smile at her daughter's earnest tone. 'What is it about?'

'Nathaniel and Lamorna.' She paused. 'They have been to Newlyn together.'

'Surely not!' Eliza was startled into serious attention. 'What makes you say so?'

'I went with Edgar to Newlyn – '

'What! Why would you do such a thing!'

'Don't be cross, Mama! I wanted a painting, a special one, for your birthday and I told Edgar and he suggested we went to see a friend of his in Newlyn who has opened a gallery and sells paintings – modern ones – at reasonable prices.' Eliza did not know whether to laugh or be angry.

'That Edgar! Sometimes he seems little older than you!' she exclaimed. 'So, what happened?'

'We went, last week, after Father was out of the way – '

'Caroline!!'

'Anyway, we went,' Caroline continued, doggedly. 'And we saw some wonderful pictures and he was such a nice man in the gallery – he knew Edgar from when he was a Revenue man – and he said lots of good artists from France were coming to Newlyn because they could reach London easily from there and – '

'Yes, yes, go on.'

And then I saw a picture of a girl on the beach. It was Lamorna, I am sure it was. And the picture was signed Nat Trevannion!'

'But Nathaniel is in school! In Exeter!'

'They have a weekend leave of absence sometimes, I know they do. The man in the gallery says that Nathaniel came several times to paint this girl on the beach. He wanted to paint from real life. But the first time the wind was too strong – but he came again – and I am sure the girl is Lamorna!'

More than ever, Eliza was relieved that Barnabas was away. She could well imagine his rage if he found out what Nathaniel had been doing. At home, their son had given no indication that he was dabbling in art, or even mildly interested. Rather the reverse. Perhaps Lamorna had intrigued him and led him down this new path, a path strewn with brambles for a young man with a father still sublimely sure that his strictures held sway over all his family. And Nathaniel had reached the age to rebel. What about Lamorna and her father? She must have found a way to avoid Austol. There was only one thing for it. She must go to Newlyn, meet this man at his gallery and find out more.

'Tis a long way – t'other side o' Penzance,' advised Mathey. 'The streets are mostly cobbled and only a few are gravel – could be a very bumpy ride.'

'No matter,' said Eliza serenely. 'I know you will do your best.'

'Going on your own, then?'

'Yes.' Mathey shook his head in disapproval. 'Mr. Barnabas wouldn't like it.'

'I know that, Mathey! That is why I am going while he is away.' The old man rolled his eyes heavenwards. Reluctantly he helped his mistress climb into the trap.

'Not leaving now, surely!' a voiced called. It was Edgar. What dreadful timing was Eliza's thought as he dismounted and came towards them.

'I'm going to Newlyn,' said Eliza, defiantly.

'In that case I shall accompany you. Mathey, could you see to my horse?'

Edgar took over the reins and the pony trotted down the long drive, Eliza uncertain whether to be cross or rather pleased that she had his company on the way. The cloud of Mathey's displeasure would have been hard to bear on a long journey. She was forced to confide in Edgar about the purpose of her visit and was not surprised when he looked uncomfortable.

'Jean Luc is a friend of mine,' he said. 'I expect Caroline told you. It was supposed to be a secret. But when we found the painting of Lamorna, that was a surprise.'

'I do not doubt it,' said Eliza, drily. 'I look forward to seeing it. But you know, Edgar, you should not have taken Caroline all the way to Newlyn without permission – or at least informing someone.'

'She is sixteen. I thought it would be in order.' He did not add that Caroline had contrived to give the impression that she was allowed to go to Newlyn.

It was a long rattling ride to Penzance; unfortunately, the beautiful viewpoint from where St. Michael's Mount could usually be seen showed it veiled in drizzle and surrounded with a sea of slate grey. Eliza was relieved. She wanted no reminders of her magical time with Seth. Reaching Penzance, they alternated potholes with cobbles and the pony huffed at the gradient of the hill through the town, Edgar encouraging it on with kindly clicks of his tongue. A brief descent to the harbour and then another long climb, ahead of them the cottages of Newlyn clinging to the slopes of a vertiginous hill like limpets to a rock. Out at sea Eliza could glimpse the sails of fishing boats, 'luggers' Edgar informed her, fishing for herring. Through a maze of narrow lanes they trotted, into a miasma of fishy smells which made Eliza clap a handkerchief over her nose.

'Fishing is their living!' Edgar informed her. 'What do you expect!'

Jean Luc lived and worked in a small, rather unimpressive cottage. He emerged, beaming, to greet Edgar. 'Bienvenu, mon vieux!' he cried, then turned to Eliza. 'Welcome to my home,' he said with great courtesy. 'Jean Luc Martigny at your service.' His snapping black eyes took her in at a glance and, fortunately, he appeared to like what he saw.

'So you are ze mother of the handsome Nathaniel,' he said. 'And you 'ave come to see his work? Why does he not paint at home? You should be proud of 'is – 'ow you say – talent. Now, do come in and taste some of my good brandy. Best French brandy, eh, Edgar?' And he went off into peals of laughter, joined rather hesitantly by Revenue man Edgar. The brandy was like silk in the mouth and fire in the throat and poor Eliza choked at her first taste, which delighted her host. He screwed up his wizened brown face with pleasure.

'I must paint you – such an expressive face, such lovely hair! I see you looking out to sea, waiting for your loved one to come home......'

'Jean Luc, we have come to see the painting of Lamorna,' interrupted Edgar.

'Ah, oui – come and see my gallery.'

The gallery was just a room which took up most of the ground floor of the cottage but the walls were covered with paintings, oils, water colours, in gouache, and sketches in many differing styles. Eliza exclaimed with pleasure.

'And here is Nat's painting!' she cried. A girl, unmistakeably Lamorna, was depicted looking out to sea from the harbour. She wore a calico apron over her dress and her hair spilled over her shoulders, ruffled by the sea breeze. The expression on her face showed a mixture of anxiety and longing and Eliza could imagine that she was looking for the return of someone dear to her.

'How clever of Nathaniel to capture that expression!' she marvelled. 'I had no idea he had reached such a level of competence. Surely they must have art lessons at his school?' Edgar shrugged his shoulders.

'I only know that Lamorna enthuses over him – but does not say anything to her father. It seems that Nathaniel does not confide in Barnabas either?'

'He is so seldom free to talk to his children,' said Eliza. 'He is away just now and when he is home he is in his study or at the mines. I do not understand,' she continued in a burst of confidence, 'He seemed so relaxed when he first came home as if money problems were in the past.'

'Maybe things have changed,' offered Edgar. 'I believe most businesses need constant attention to succeed and he and Seth Quinn seem to be working on new and difficult ideas in Wheal Rose.'

'Wheal Rose!' cried Eliza. 'Is that its name? I did not know.' Quite illogically she felt hurt.

'Wheal Eliza exists already,' said Edgar lightly, conscious that he might have betrayed a confidence. 'Seth Quinn told me and I thought Barnabas would have told you.' Eliza nodded and returned to scrutinising the picture, unwilling to reveal the depth of her wounded feelings. Of course Seth would like to call the mine by his wife's name, it would be small minded to resent that. But neither he nor Barnabas had seen fit to tell her, to take her into their confidence.

'I 'ave another picture of ze girl,' Jean Luc said. He took Eliza's arm and conducted her along the row of canvases till they came to an oil of a girl sitting on a chair outside a door. No wistful expression but one of defiance, her hat rammed on her head and her fists clenched. But again, it was Lamorna. No mistake.

'Both these pictures were painted 'en plein air' announced Jean Luc. 'Luckily ze weather was good.'

'Has Lamorna done any paintings for you?' asked Eliza, remembering the powerful green and blue abstract she had shown them. Jean Luc frowned.

'She say that she will show me her work when she 'as had lessons in Londres, not before.'

'She is good already.' Eliza murmured.

She and Edgar wandered down to the beach, just a stone's throw from Jean Luc's cottage. The tide was still going out, revealing stretches of shiny sand and shingle. Busily, like many coloured moths, the fishing boats seemed to flutter over the sea, followed by flocks of gulls wheeling and diving.

'I understand Nathaniel wanting to paint in such a place,' murmured Eliza. 'But why did he not tell us?' Edgar shrugged his shoulders in a Gallic way.

'He is growing up – and wants a life of his own?' He deftly changed the subject. 'Now I feel that another sip of that brandy will help us on the long journey back!'

11

'Edgar – have you nothing better to do than keep visiting us?' demanded Eliza, failing to hide her irritation. 'I am always pleased to see you, you know that, but I have the feeling that you are again bearing a message from Austol?'

'Yes, I am, but I always enjoy coming to Roscarne. The Manor is sometimes stifling,' admitted Edgar. Eliza laughed.

'You had better come into the morning room. Barnabas has some members of his consortium in the drawing room and goodness knows when they will finish putting the mining world to rights.'

She settled Edgar into a comfortable chair and looked at him closely.

'You do seem so much better, you know. I was worried that all that business with Samuel Hooper was going to make you ill.'

'It's like a bad dream, now, and I think of it much less,' said Edgar.

'That's good news then. Now what does Austol want this time?'

'I'm not sure how you will receive this.' Edgar cleared his throat and the words came out in a rush. 'He wants Jean Luc to paint your portrait. Furthermore he wants to hang it at the Manor!' There was a pause as Eliza digested this unexpected request.

'That is out of the question!' she exclaimed at last. 'I am not his wife – or any other close relation! What on earth would people think! Besides, Barnabas would never agree. I am really shocked that Austol should entertain such an idea.'

She shook her head in bewilderment. Edgar did not look surprised but continued doggedly.

'Austol declares that he is particularly enthusiastic about portrait painting and he feels you have an interesting face. He would like to add you to his collection.'

'Would he indeed!' said Eliza, caustically, then querying 'How does he know Jean Luc?'

'I made the mistake of telling him about Newlyn and all the artists there – and my friendship with Jean Luc – and that seemed to give him the idea.'

'Does he know Nathaniel and Lamorna have been to Newlyn?'

'Yes, I'm afraid so.' Edgar looked suitably contrite. Then he brightened. 'I think Austol is willing to accept an art school in Penzance for Lamorna if it distracts her from the idea of going to London.'

'He should get Jean Luc to paint Lamorna then. What has it all to do with me?'

'Nathaniel?' said Edgar delicately.

After Edgar had taken his leave, bearing an uncompromising refusal from Eliza, she remained curled up in her chair, deep in thought. How was she to disentangle herself from Austol's continual demands? She was feeling even more harassed and knew that he would not give up lightly. Perhaps she had been naïve, as Seth pointed out, and she should not have involved herself in the daily life of the Manor. She gazed moodily out of the window and it was there Barnabas found her. He bounded in, full of good cheer. His meeting had obviously gone well. Eliza told him about Austol's request and the smile left his face.

'I am not sure that would be proper,' he growled.

'Neither am I,' agreed Eliza. 'But how will my refusal affect Austol's entry into the consortium? He might take it badly and refuse to join.'

'That is a possibility,' agreed Barnabas. 'But a portrait of my wife is not going to grace the walls of the

Manor! And if he does not want to join the consortium we shall manage without him.' However Eliza observed that a shadow had darkened his face. Perhaps managing without him would not be so easy. However Barnabas' words gave her an idea. 'That's it! Grace! He should paint Grace – after all she is the beautiful one!'

'Sometimes I despair of you, Eliza,' said her husband. 'You are the one with vivacity and animation! You are not a porcelain doll and all the more attractive for that! In fact Austol demonstrates remarkably good taste in choosing you as a model.'

Eliza gazed at him in astonishment. It was a long time since a compliment had come her way from Barnabas. Perhaps the attention she had received from Austol had revived his appreciation.

'Thank you, Barnabas,' she said demurely. Barnabas looked slightly surprised at his own words. Of course his wife was much more personable than her sister, dammit, not just personable but attractive. Even beautiful. He noted her fall of dark hair, hair which should have been put up but of course she did not have a maid of her own. Her complexion was clear and blushed with palest pink, swept by her dark lashes. Her waist was still trim in spite of their brood of children and her hands had recovered from her time at Carnglaze. More than that, he knew she was intelligent, sometimes impulsive, sometimes argumentative, but he recognised his good fortune in possessing her as his wife, regretting that he was often too busy to take time and enjoy what he had. It was a pity there were so many other concerns to worry about, which took up his time and energy.

It was the same evening, an evening of sudden squalls which ruffled the surface of the sea and made the windows rattle, that again Eliza found her world shaken by Barnabas. They were all gathered in the drawing room waiting for supper and chatting desultorily. Seth was making himself agreeable to Uncle Tobias while Rose and Eliza were discussing

Caroline's new dress. Grace was late, but when she did arrive she attached herself to the master of the, house, enquiring earnestly if Barnabas had been to Paris recently. Eliza stifled a giggle at her husband's perplexed face. Then Ewella came in.

'Someone to see you,' she said to Barnabas. 'A young lady.' Her tone mixed curiosity with disapproval. Eliza observed the fleeting shock with which Barnabas reacted to this news.

'Late for an afternoon call,' said Rose.

'It cannot be someone from the consortium,' put in Caroline. 'Ladies are not allowed to belong – yet!' Eliza found she could not utter a word. A sense of foreboding gripped her as she waited for the return of her husband.

The minutes ticked by. Then at last he appeared, escorting the visitor into the room.

'This is Miss Selena Bawden,' he announced. 'I have invited her to stay for supper and Ewella is just going to lay another place.' All eyes turned to Miss Selena. She stood modestly next to Barnabas, her head bowed as if unwilling to face the combined scrutiny of so many people. Her heavy, blue black hair fell forward, hiding her features. A much washed shawl was draped over her thin shoulders and her dress was muddied at the hem.

'She looks about eighteen,' said Rose in an undertone. 'What is she doing on her own so far from Rosmorren at this time of day?' There was silence as everyone took their place in the dining table. Then Uncle Tobias smiled at Miss Bawden and, utilising one of the prerogatives of old age, asked her directly where she was from.

'Falmouth,' she whispered. 'I was living with my mother but she died. Everyone murmured their sympathy.

'Have you any relatives left in Falmouth?' Uncle Tobias continued.

'No. The only person I know in the whole of Cornwall is Mr. Trevannion so I have come to visit him. I am hoping he will help me to settle somewhere – '

Questions were buzzing like bees in the heads of those present but Barnabas held up his hand.

'I think we should leave our visitor time to taste her soup,' he smiled.

Eliza noticed that behind the polite smiles, her husband was strained and a pulse was beating in his forehead.

Rose and Seth retired early to their room, feeling that they were in the way. Uncle Tobias hobbled off to his study realising that he would not be allowed to question Miss Selena any further. Eliza would have liked Caroline to go to her room but her daughter remained grimly attached to her chair. She wanted to know more. Who was this girl and how did she know her father? She would not leave until she found out.

'How did you travel here, Miss Selena?' asked Eliza gently. 'It will soon be dark and it is a long way to Falmouth.'

'I was given a lift in the Exeter coach,' the girl answered briefly

'That's a long ride,' said Caroline. 'The horses must get so tired.'

'Not just the horses,' said Barnabas, in reproof. 'A long ride for anyone. Miss Selena will have to stay here overnight. It is out of the question for her to travel back on her own.' Without missing a beat, Eliza rose.

'I shall go to see Ewella and arrange for a room to be made ready.' Outside the door she paused for breath. What was the matter with her? The poor girl had lost her mother and what was more natural than that she seek out someone she knew. But how did she know Barnabas? He had never mentioned a Miss Selena Bawden even though he had visited Falmouth fairly often since his return from his travels. Try as she might, Eliza could not dismiss this visitation as of no account. She needed to know more.

'I hardly know her,' said Barnabas, later. 'Her mother used to take in lodgers and I stayed there a few times and I knew she had a daughter but did not see much of her. Now she has been left entirely on her own and does not know what to do.'

'Poor girl,' said Eliza, genuinely moved by the plight of someone so young.

'I hoped you would feel like that,' said Barnabas eagerly. 'I think we might be able to help her. She will need employment and perhaps she could find it here. Eliza, did you not say you wanted a lady's maid? Selena would be able to do that!' Not Miss Selena or even Mistress Bawden. A stunned Eliza did not know what to say.

12

Miss Selena was absorbed slowly into the day to day life of Roscarne, as not everyone was comfortable with her presence. Uncle Tobias in particular was disapproving, wondering out loud how anyone could be left with no relatives and no friends.

'I do not need a lady's maid,' said Eliza, having had time to think. 'I'm sure you could find her something else to do if she wishes to pay her way. How long do you envisage she will be here with us?' Barnabas shrugged his shoulders.

'We cannot throw the poor girl out. She and her mother were very good to me when I returned from Australia. I stayed with them for some time.'

'Why did you not come straight home?'

'I was ill. I did not want to return to you in such a state. Prison in Australia did not do much for my general health.'

'Carnglaze did not improve our health either!' snapped Eliza. 'The worst thing of all was wondering if you really WERE coming back. And poor Uncle Tobias was drooping and diminishing before our eyes!' Barnabas laughed, much to Eliza's irritation.

'Did you see how much he ate at suppertime? He won't be 'diminishing' anymore!'

The problem of Miss Selena was solved when Nanny Hannah announced that she wanted babies to look after, not grown children, and a friend back in Devon had just given birth to twins and needed assistance

'Of course I shall miss Elestren and Richard very much,' she said, earnestly. 'But perhaps I may come back to visit them occasionally?'

'Of course, of course,' said Barnabas, heartily. Grace was not so pleased.

'I rely on Nanny Hannah,' she said, sulkily. 'She does my hair and sees to my clothes. Then there's Elestren. Who will look after her?'

'She IS nearly six years old,' said Eliza, soothingly. 'I am sure you can manage. She will do her lessons with Miss Maisie as before. Of course Caroline, Richard, Nessa and Joel will be here for her so she will not take up much of your energy.' Privately she vowed to spend extra time with Elestren herself; Grace was not to be trusted to give her children the care they needed. Her main concern was her own well-being and when she was lost in her hazy world of shadows she did not always recognise them as her responsibility. Fortunately the sedative medication Dr. Trevell had left for her seemed to have calmed her violent outbursts, though the children were instructed not to visit her alone.

Miss Selena was given Nanny Hannah's room and earned Grace's immediate approval by proving to be a competent lady's maid. She would coil Grace's blonde hair into becoming styles, massage her shoulders when she threatened to become hysterical and scurry up and down stairs with armfuls of dresses she insisted on ironing herself, using the heavy pressing irons in the basement. When Grace could not sleep she sat with her, reading to her or just talking quietly until Grace's eyelids closed. Even Richard could not fault her care for his mother.

'She reads very well,' he said to Eliza. 'And I did not expect her to know so much. She is not really like a lady's maid at all.'

'No, she's not,' said Eliza, thoughtfully.

Caroline, however, was not happy. 'Mama, I feel that she has cast a blight over this house. It's like a squall is expected.

Even when it is a fine day the sun does not seem to reach us. Now Father has insisted she takes her meals with us – unheard of for a lady's maid – and conversation has become stilted and – and not real.'

'I am puzzled about that,' admitted Eliza. 'But your father insists that he was treated so well in Falmouth that it would be unthinkable to relegate her to the kitchen with Mrs. Adwyn and the other maids.'

Caroline, curled on a window-seat in the morning room, looked unconvinced.

'I wonder what Austol will think of her,' she murmured. 'When is he coming to supper next?'

'He is bringing Lamorna – oh, and Edgar – next week.'

'I hope they have decided what to do about finding an art school for Lamorna,' Caroline added. 'Otherwise there will be another disagreeable evening in store.'

The next morning, a heavily perfumed letter arrived from Aunt Gloria, announcing her imminent arrival and apologising for the short notice.

'I have had no news of you all for some time,' she wrote in her distinctive, slanting hand, which did not betray any of the tremors of old age. 'However,' she went on, 'I would be remiss not to see you now you are safely back at Roscarne. As you probably realise, I have only just heard the full, horrifying story of your stay at Carnglaze – how could you not tell me before? I would have been delighted to help!'

'WHO told Aunt Gloria?' lamented Eliza to Rose. 'I did not want her to feel responsible for us any more – she has done so much already!'

'She would have wanted to help you by giving you money,' said Rose, adding with a smile, 'But you can't throw money at ghosts!'

'That is true,' agreed Eliza. 'But knowing Aunt Gloria, she would have given her last penny to see us move to

another house. And she has her own troubles – having lost
Yelland and suffering with poor health herself.'

Barnabas was absent from the supper planned for Austol,
declaring that he was going to Exeter to see Nathaniel. Eliza
was torn between anger and relief, anger that he had left her to
Austol's mercy again and relief that one cause of contention
had been removed. Seth willingly agreed to meet Aunt Gloria
and escort her from the London coach to Roscarne on the very
same day as the supper. Eliza wondered gloomily what Aunt
Gloria would make of the assembled company. No Barnabas,
Seth and Rose living there, Caroline old enough to join them
at table and – Selena. Then the guests, Austol, Edgar, Kenwyn
and Lamorna. Her antennae would be quivering with
curiosity. Still, it would be wonderful to see her again so
apprehension was mixed with pleasure at the prospect.

The night of the supper was dry though clouds lined the
horizon and the sea had turned indigo. With the heavy
curtains drawn and the silver mirroring the flames of many
candles, Eliza could be proud of the dining room. In her best
claret silk and a lacy shawl, she made an attractive hostess and
the knowledge that she was looking her best gave her courage.

Aunt Gloria's arrival caused a stir. Seth flung the door open
for her and she entered like a duchess in a swirl of powder and
perfume.
        'I have not seen you all for so long!' she cried as
everyone took turns to greet her. 'Tobias, you look younger
than ever! And Caroline – so tall and elegant! And who is
this, pray?'
        'This is Miss Selena who is staying with us,' said
Eliza, flustered. Aunt Gloria's eyebrows rose but just then
Austol arrived with Edgar, Kenwyn and Lamorna jostling
behind him. Austol was in haughty lord of the manor mode
but nevertheless paid great attention to Aunt Gloria which
pleased that lady. Caroline and Lamorna chattered together

happily and the only jarring note was the way Seth glowered at Edgar, who appeared not to notice.

After supper the gentlemen retired to smoke and drink brandy while Aunt Gloria cornered Eliza to find out what was happening.

'I am so pleased that you and Rose are reunited,' she said. There followed a barrage of questions. 'But where is Barnabas and who is this Miss Selena? Why is she staying here? And you must tell me all about Carnglaze! I heard gossip that it was a haunted house! Is that true?' Eliza recounted some of the story of their stay in Carnglaze, omitting the more frightening details and then recruited Rose to tell her all about Arizona.

With everyone engaged in conversation, Eliza slipped out. Her face was burning. It was always difficult to divert Aunt Gloria and her questions were shrewd.

'Mrs. Adwyn, I have come to beg you for a glass of cold water,' she said. 'And, of course, to thank you for a wonderful meal. The squab pies were your best.' The cook smiled in pleasure. Mistress Eliza was always generous with her praise.

Eliza took the glass of water and went to stand by the window in the passageway. This looked out over the moor, lit by a moon as bright as a silver penny. As she gazed, entranced, she was suddenly conscious of another presence. With a shock, she realised it was Seth.

'We have not spoken to each other lately,' he whispered. 'I miss you.' They stood close to each other, neither with the power to move away. Gently Seth put his hand on her neck and kissed her cheek, an act which seemed to fire them both. She found herself in his arms and they kissed wildly, with no thought of anyone else. Then Seth dragged himself away and Eliza felt again that the plaited skeins of silk binding them so closely were tearing.

'Eliza, I am so sorry. I should not have behaved like that. Please forgive me.' He stroked her hair briefly and left her. She stood by the window, trying to calm her breathing and gather herself together for her return to her guests.

'Well, Miss Eliza, I am surprised to find you here. Or perhaps not. Mr. Quinn has just returned to the drawing room.' It was Austol's dry tones.

13

Back in the drawing room, Eliza, longing desperately for the evening to end, tried to enter into the general conversation. The gentlemen had returned to join the ladies and all the time she was conscious of Austol sitting opposite her with a quizzical look on his face. Had he really seen them? Or had he jumped to conclusions? Seth was immersed in a discussion with Uncle Tobias and made a point of not looking her way, his shoulders rigid as the only sign of the stress he was under.

Meanwhile Aunt Gloria was probing poor Rose about the state of her health; at the same time she observed that her elder niece was jumpy and nervous. This would need looking in to. It was so strange the way this household had changed. Surely another family, not related, should not be staying at Roscarne? Why was Austol Treloyhan always around? And that Miss Selena? She had not received a satisfactory explanation for her presence from Eliza. Then what about the master of the house? Barnabas? Where was he?

No sooner had Aunt Gloria retired to her room amidst a chorus of respectful good wishes for a peaceful night when Lamorna appeared at Eliza's side.

'Oh Mistress Eliza,' she whispered. 'I am worried about Nathaniel. I know that Mr. Trevannion is going to see him. What is going to happen?' Eliza realised how pale Austol's daughter appeared, how her features had sharpened even more.

'I really do not know,' she whispered back. 'But I am sure Nathaniel and his father will have a sensible talk.

However, I do think you two should have asked permission for your outings.'

'Then we would have had no chance! My father would never have allowed us to meet or go to Newlyn and I fear Mr. Trevannion would feel the same way!' A statement with which Eliza was forced to agree.

'Lamorna! Your father wants you. Now!'

Lamorna made a face and scurried out, leaving Edgar, who had been vying for Eliza's attention.

'Miss Eliza,' he said urgently, in low tones. 'Austol says he is expecting you to take tea with him tomorrow!'

'Tomorrow?' snapped Eliza. 'Aunt Gloria is staying. That will not be possible.'

'Austol says it is important and he will be expecting you.' Edgar looked awkward, then hurried off.

So Eliza found herself opposite Austol, much against her will, in that deep chair of his with such high arms that she felt she was immured in a prison cell.

'Austol, what is so important? I should not be here. Aunt Gloria is with us and cannot stay for long!'

'My dear, I shall not keep you. I just needed to establish that we understand one another.' Austol's voice slithered over her like a snake. Eliza repressed a shudder. She knew what he meant. Oh yes, she understood him only too well.

'I was beginning to think that you were a marble maiden – perhaps not a maiden –' he laughed at his own joke. 'But having realised that you are, how shall I phrase it, not quite perfect – I feel that your husband would be most interested to know what was happening – ' He raised one eyebrow. With difficulty, Eliza stood up.

'Austol, I do not care for you to speak to me in this way. In any case, problems in my family are no business of yours – '

'You are mistaken!' Austol interrupted, his voice turning harsh. 'Lamorna is involved with your family in a way that is of great concern to me. I shall discipline her and I trust you will see that Barnabas does the same with Nathaniel. I am sure you realise that I do not intend to belong to a consortium or invest my money in Wheal Rose if matters stand as they are.'

Eliza felt the colour leaving her face. So Austol was threatening her on two counts. He could destroy her marriage and damage Barnabas' mining interests. Then she would be instrumental in hurting Rose and losing Seth as well. Her mind could easily comprehend all the destruction that lay ahead. Her children, Uncle Tobias and of course, Roscarne!

'Eliza, my dear,' Austol swooped to put an arm about her. 'Do not look so stricken! I do not wish to harm you. Your secret is safe with me! Come now, we shall have some brandy and that will make you feel better. I promise you it is very good brandy straight from France – though Edgar does disapprove of the way I obtain it.' Austol laughed genially as he grasped Eliza's arm and propelled her to the drawing room where he kept a large mahogany cabinet full of various bottles, including the much vaunted brandy.

Edgar drove a silent Eliza back to Roscarne in the pony and trap. His concern for her grew with each mile; she was pale as candlewax and her eyes were shadowed. Damn Austol for causing such distress in someone for whom he felt affection and admiration in equal parts, admiration for the way she had borne her other trials with such fortitude, particularly during their time at Carnglaze, being faced with a derelict house, no husband, all the children and a difficult sister – not to mention unquiet spirits. Talking to Rose had enlightened him on their past troubles, going back to the times when they had both lost their parents and when Eliza had married Barnabas, which also brought difficulties.

'Mistress Eliza, can I help in any way?' he ventured but she turned her violet eyes on him, eyes glassy with tears and shook her head.

'Edgar, you have been so kind to me – and I do not deserve it. I have made mistakes and I have to pay for them, it is as simple as that. There is nothing anyone can do. I have to sort it all out myself.'

Eliza arrived at Roscarne to find Barnabas simmering with rage.

'I am so pleased that you find time to spare for your family at Roscarne! You seem to spend more time at the Manor catering to Austol's whims than you do here!'

Eliza reeled under the sudden attack and then retorted with spirit:

'And you, Barnabas, you spend more time away from your home than you spend in it! Why should I not have a similar freedom?' Barnabas almost choked with anger at this temerity.

'Because you are my wife! You have responsibilities in this house that you profess to love so much! Is there any wonder that Ewella is struggling to keep everything organised on her own! And that your children are running wild!'

'What DO you mean?'

'I gather that Joel kicked Miss Maisie?' This was undeniable.

'And now Nathaniel has announced that he wishes to leave school and take up art! I ask you, what kind of a calling is that? Strutting around in peculiar clothes and mixing with ladies of doubtful reputation in order to paint pictures! And, I believe, involving Lamorna with his silly ideas!'

'I think it is more likely that Lamorna involved HIM,' said Eliza. 'In any case, you have to remember that Nathaniel is growing up. At nearly seventeen he is not a child anymore.' There was silence as Barnabas digested this. She pursued her advantage.

'Lamorna has real talent. Without doubt she will become a famous painter. Nathaniel is lucky to know her.' Barnabas fixed his fierce blue eyes on her.

'How can you possibly make such a wild assessment on the basis of seeing a few pictures?'

'Barnabas, please come on our next visit to Austol and see what Lamorna has done! Also kindly remember that you asked me to avoid displeasing Austol as you hope to retain his interest in your consortium!' I have tried to do so but I have found it no easy task!' This silenced her husband.

There was a tap at the door and Selena came in. She ignored Eliza and went straight to Barnabas, wringing her hands in a theatrical way, or so Eliza thought.

'Oh Barnabas – I mean Mr. Barnabas –' she amended hastily. 'Mistress Grace is in one of her tantrums and said I was to leave her room! She threw her brushes at me and said she never wanted to see me again!' And she burst into loud hiccupping sobs. No tears, noticed Eliza.

''Please do not distress yourself, my dear Selena,' replied the master of the house. 'She will have forgotten all about it in an hour or two. Mistress Eliza here will give you other duties meanwhile. I have to leave – meetings you know.' He disappeared at speed, leaving Eliza to deal with a distraught Selena. The girl turned to Eliza, giving her a look that was at once disparaging and mutinous, an attitude that was a far cry from her earlier modest demeanour. It was noticeable that there were no tears in her eyes.

'Perhaps you would like to have a break from 'duties' and go to Mrs. Adwyn in the kitchen and have some tea?' suggested Eliza.

'I don't want you to be kind to me!' Selena cried. 'Mr. Barnabas can tell me what to do! Not you!'

'As I am mistress of this house, I, too, can tell you what to do,' said Eliza, in mild tones.

'But Ewella said – '

'And what did Ewella say?'

'She said that you were not – oh, what does it matter!' Selena had obviously realised that she could be in real trouble.

She looked around her wildly and then dashed out of the door, leaving behind a puzzled Eliza.

14

An improvement in the weather elicited an improvement in the atmosphere within Roscarne. Selena and Grace had obviously been reconciled, Ewella was unusually cheerful and Barnabas had made no mention of his planned visit to Exeter.
'I shall call in to see Nathaniel the next time I go,' he said airily, when Eliza tackled him.
This was a change in attitude! Perhaps he was avoiding a confrontation with his eldest son? She could only surmise. He seemed cheerful and did not make a fuss when Eliza announced her intention of visiting the Manor the following week.
'I shall not accompany you. I have important meetings and do not wish to spend any free time I have with Austol and his gaggle of daughters. I am sure Mathey will be able to drive you.'

'Eliza, Seth has had such a good idea! He has promised to take me to St. Michael's Mount if the weather holds. Please do come with us – it should be such an interesting outing.'
Rose was full of excitement at the prospect. Eliza was brought up short. St. Michael's Mount? Where Seth had promised to take her one day. So, he intended to take Rose instead?'
'Seth said he thought you would like to walk over the causeway and visit the castle,' prattled Rose. 'Please do come!'
'We should both enjoy your company,' Seth said later, avoiding Eliza's gaze. Well, why not?
It would not be feasible for her to go with him alone as well she knew. It was childish of her to expect it. Men were so

much more pragmatic in the face of difficult choices and he was no different from all the rest.

'I should love to come with you both,' Eliza said brightly. But fate had other plans.

The morning of the proposed visit was cloudless, an auspicious beginning. However, Rose reached only as far as the front door before collapsing with a megrim. She took to her bed, moaning softly that they should go anyway and take advantage of the fine weather.

'I cannot leave you like this,' said Seth, anxiously.

'There is nothing to be done for me – you know that. I have to sleep it off.'

'Such an outing will do you good,' said Barnabas heartily to Eliza. 'You have been looking pale recently. Do not worry about Rose. Ewella will take care of her.'

'I wonder if such an outing is quite – quite proper?' queried Eliza.

'I am your husband and I give you permission! Who will argue with me?' Eliza fell silent. She found it strange that Barnabas was being so accommodating.

'We shall go again when you are better,' Seth promised his wife.

So he and Eliza found themselves bowling along the road to Penzance, gloriously free, though neither one of them referred to this fortuitous turn of events. In fact conversation was at a minimum, each deep in their thoughts. Eliza, for her part, felt an awkwardness that she had not experienced before. She wondered if Seth felt the same.

A benign sun, denying the approach of winter, lit up the pale yellow sands of Marazion. Ahead of them, like a mirage, St. Michael's Mount rose out of a glittering sea, magical and unattainable. The beauty of it caught in Eliza's throat and she could not speak. Seth was less overcome. Peeved, he realised that the tide was in far enough to cover the causeway and make it impossible to cross. It was still rising and to wait for the cobblestones to appear again would obviously be a waste of hours. How could he have been so remiss?

'Don't be angry, Seth,' said Eliza. 'Just to see this place is a marvellous experience. We can come again sometime, but for me the sight of it on this beautiful day has given me such pleasure.'

Seth stopped glowering and smiled at Eliza. How accepting of rebuffs and disappointments she was proving to be. And there she was, sitting close to him, her cheeks pink in the sun, her hair escaping from her bonnet and her eyes wide with enjoyment.

'Where else shall we go?' she demanded, deftly preventing any suggestion that they return to Roscarne. Seth laughed, well aware of her thoughts.

'I think we should make the most of our sudden freedom!' he said. 'I shall take you to Newlyn instead and you can show me Nathaniel's paintings.'

'I like that idea,' smiled Eliza. 'But perhaps we could have our picnic first? It has been a long way here and I expect the pony is tired.'

'I shall tether the pony and we can walk along the beach to find a suitable spot,' agreed Seth. 'And we shall still have a view of the castle.'

'And the sun is still out,' Eliza said happily.

Further along, away from the few people out on the sand, they found the perfect spot, sheltered by sand dunes and backed by a granite wall. Seth unrolled the blanket he was carrying.

'This should be to wrap round you in the trap,' he smiled. 'But it will do very well as a tablecloth.' He laid it on the sand while Eliza unpacked her basket.

'We have new baked bread, cheese and saffron biscuits, – ooh – and apples,' she reported. 'Ewella has been kind. Though I do not think she would approve of us having a picnic on the sand like this.'

'She would not approve at all,' agreed Seth with a wicked grin.

Later, sleepy with sun and saffron biscuits, they leaned back against the sand dune.
'I am surprised that Barnabas let you come with me after Rose dropped out,' mused Seth. 'I know you are a respectable married matron and not a young girl, but I am still puzzled why he should allow it. I would not have done!'
'I know Barnabas does not conform to convention. He does what he wants to do and perhaps he thinks that I should have the same freedom.'
'There I think you misjudge him. He seems to trust me but he does not like you going to visit Austol. He is always displeased when he finds out you have gone there.'
'There YOU misjudge him. He is glad that I help Austol with his girls and household problems because then Austol feels indebted and is more likely to invest in Wheal Rose.'
'I cannot believe Barnabas would have such a motive!' Seth sounded genuinely shocked. 'To use you in that way is scandalous!'
'We have been married for a long time,' said Eliza, tiredly. 'He sees me as the mother of his children, as a housekeeper, as a nurse for Uncle Tobias – but as a wife? I think not. I feel his first love is mining and the consortium. Mining matters, good or bad, take him over, occupy his time, enthuse him or worry him and he has no time for me.'
To her chagrin, she felt the tears well up and a sob escaped her.
'Oh Eliza, I would never treat you like that!' Seth gathered her into his arms. She pushed him away, anger chasing away the tears.
'You treated me more cruelly than that! You told me that you loved me and yet you married Rose! And then you ran away to Arizona!'

'I explained why!' Seth protested. 'I needed some distance. You are married to a man I am proud to call my friend and who has always treated me with generosity and kindness. Then I repay him by falling in love with his wife! What kind of man does that make me?'

'The kind of man I am stupid enough to fall in love with!' said Eliza.

'At least we have established that we are in love with each other.' A grin broke through and Seth's dark eyes lost their sombre look.

'Let us make the most of the sunshine and the time we have together!' Before Eliza could protest he caught her in his arms again and kissed her. For a brief moment she resisted then, with a sigh, collapsed against him. She had tried to keep her distance, tried to maintain a cool but friendly manner towards him, tried to remember Rose – but she found herself overwhelmed by feelings long repressed. The surrounding sky, the yellow sand, the slapping wavelets of the incoming tide were of no consequence, her world had room only for the man beside her. The feel of his skin, of his lips, the tautness of his body were the stuff of her dreams and she knew she would never forget this time with him.

Seth awoke first. His movement alerted Eliza and she scrambled into a sitting position, exclaiming that her dress was so creased! Ewella would never believe that the ride in the trap did all that.

'No, I did all that,' said Seth complacently. 'And it is my fault that your hair is all over your shoulders and that is how I like it.' That made Eliza laugh.

The sun, a winter sun, was setting so they decided a prompt return to Roscarne was needed. The temperature was dropping and the blue of the sky had dulled to grey. Solicitously, Seth shook out the sand and wrapped the blanket round Eliza.

'We shall come again,' he promised. 'I wish to meet Edgar's friend from Brittany and see the paintings.'

'AND cross the causeway when the tide is out!' giggled Eliza. Neither of them referred to the fact that obviously Rose would accompany them and the outings would be very different. The pony had revived after its long rest and trotted with alacrity on the way homeward.

'I do hope Rose's megrim has improved,' ventured Eliza as, finally, they reached Roscarne and trotted up the long drive. Mathey appeared to rub down and feed the pony, looking quite surprised to see just the two of them.

'Visitors d'ave come to see you,' he said.

'Not Austol I hope,' whispered Eliza. It was not Austol. The Tregadilletts had come to visit Grace. They were seated with her in the drawing room when Eliza and Seth entered. No sign of Rose or Barnabas. Morwenna could hardly believe her eyes.

'Is Mr. Trevannion not with you? Nor Mistress Quinn?' Her sharp little nose was quivering with excitement. What a juicy piece of news to pass on to her friends!

'My wife is indisposed with a megrim' said Seth, shortly. 'If you will excuse me I wish to see how she is faring.' He left the room without glancing again at Eliza. She felt that she had been left in a cage of lions – no, not lions, hyenas.

It was Barnabas who saved the day. He strode in to greet the Tregadilletts and to check that Grace was in civilised mood, but was surprised to find his wife sitting there.

'Oh Mr. Trevannion did you not go on the trip to St. Michael's Mount?' trilled Morwenna.

'Such a picturesque place,' Nicholas Tregadillett said, heaving himself out of his armchair where he had nearly succumbed to sleep.

'Unfortunately I had business commitments,' was the bland reply. 'But Seth Quinn offered to escort the ladies there and I was most relieved. Even more relieved when he agreed to take Eliza even though Rose was indisposed. I had been feeling that it was time my wife escaped the house and all her domestic chores. She has been looking a little peaky recently.' Barnabas smiled kindly at Eliza.

Morwenna looked disappointed that Seth and Eliza had been given permission for their trip. Eliza realised that Barnabas had saved the day and well he knew it, giving his wife a wicked wink as he left the drawing room.

15

True winter had set in. Gone were the gentler days when the sun shone in a way reminiscent of early autumn; it still shone but from a hard, crystalline sky swept by a bitter east wind. Grace, out for a walk, returned early with pink nose and icy hands while Mrs. Adwyn, in the kitchen, decided that a warming stew would be needed for supper. Uncle Tobias evinced a desire to hibernate by retreating to his study and, wrapped in a blanket, refused to reappear for lunch. Ewella added her grumbles.

'I did not expect it to be cold so early. You would think these granite walls would hold in the warmth but not a bit of it! I was never this cold in Liskeard!'

'I expect it was so long ago you don't remember,' said Joel, not intending to be rude. His remark earned him a frosty look, however, and he marched off to the schoolroom muttering about bad tempered old ladies who took things the wrong way. Miss Maisie asked him why he was so cross but he deemed it wiser to stay mute.

The cold had not yet lifted in the schoolroom so Miss Maisie allowed them all to huddle round the fire and practise reading. Joel hid behind his book, pretending to read, but allowing his mind to wander into the delights of mining. He had inveigled his father into taking him to Wheal Eliza and he had never forgotten the buildings, the machines, the black depths accessed by cages, the miners with candle stubs in their hats, the balmaidens hefting hammers over their heads to break up the rock – and the chimneys! Those tall chimneys announcing proudly the presence of a tin mine. Joel determined that he would be a miner when he was old enough.

'I do miss Nathaniel and John,' whispered Caroline. Nessa nodded her head.

'They will be back soon for the holidays,' she said.

Barnabas and Seth returned from a visit to Wheal Rose, arriving in a blast of cold air. Seth hardly spared a glance for Eliza but hurried upstairs to see Rose who was laid low again, this time by a cold. Eliza could not avoid the flash of jealousy that assailed her. It was always Rose who received the most of his attention. Aware that she was being unreasonable, and cross with herself, she decided to forget him and write to Aunt Gloria. Hardly had she settled in the morning room and written her first lines when the door was flung open and Seth appeared.

'Where is Barnabas?' he demanded. 'Rose is not there and we must search for her.'

'Are you sure she is not in the house? She may be with Grace or with Miss Maisie in the schoolroom.'

'Ewella saw her go out and the silly woman did not try to stop her!'

'I think Rose would resent any curtailing of her movements,' said Eliza, coolly. 'But I will go and find Barnabas while you check in the rhododendron garden. I know she likes walking there.'

Mathey, however, told Eliza that Barnabas had just taken Miss Selena to Rosmorren in the pony and trap.

'I hope they freeze!' was Eliza's uncharitable thought.

Well muffled in her thickest cape she joined Seth and explained where Barnabas had gone.

'I shall help you search,' she said tersely. 'If she is not in the gardens we shall have to go down to the sea.'

'Would she go down there?' said Seth

'She is your wife!' snapped Eliza. 'You should know!' Seth looked at her in surprise, opened his mouth to say something but thought better of it. In silence they descended the path and began calling for Rose, checking the caves as they went. There was no sign of her.

'I cannot believe she would just take herself off like this,' Seth said irritably. 'I think we should go back. There is no sign of her along here.'

Ewella met them as they entered the kitchen door.

'Richard found Mistress Rose,' she announced. 'She was up in one of the attics. He said she often goes up there just to see the view.'

'That I understand,' said Eliza. Seth did not wait but bolted up the stairs to find his wife, leaving Eliza wondering why she had allowed herself to become embroiled in such an unsatisfactory situation. She was torn two ways. She enjoyed Rose's friendship and presence in Roscarne but felt continually guilty about her feelings for Seth. Yes, Seth had declared that he loved her – yet his first concern was always Rose and that hurt. Then there was the problem of Austol. He had realised that she and Seth were closer than they should be and, further, had hinted slyly that he would reveal their secret if – if what?

As if she had called up a demon by the mere mention of his name, Ewella announced that Lord Treloyhan had come to visit. Impatiently he shouldered his way into the room and it was clear he was in a rage about something.

'Eliza! Mistress Eliza! Are you aware that Lamorna and Nathaniel have run away to London without a word to me – or to you?'

'When did this happen?' stuttered Eliza.

'Yesterday! And I only found out because Edgar is incapable of keeping what he knows to himself. I take it you know nothing of their plans?'

'Nothing.'

'I should like to speak to Barnabas!'

'So should I,' thought Eliza. Aloud she said, 'That will not be possible. He has gone to Rosmorren.' Pride kept her from adding that he had taken Miss Selena – without a word to her.

Austol threw himself into an armchair.

'I shall have to wait for him,' he scowled.

'I believe Lord Treloyhan will be staying for lunch,' Eliza reported to Ewella and Mrs. Adwyn. Glumly she returned to the morning room to offer Austol some refreshment while they were waiting but found that he was chatting amiably to Seth. She left them to it. She would talk to Caroline and see how much she knew of her twin's intentions.

'They have run away?' Caroline turned putty coloured. Poor Caroline. It was clear she knew nothing of Nathaniel's movements or involvements.

'That Lamorna!' she burst out. 'She is leading Nathaniel astray! He is my brother, not hers! Maybe that is why I have been having strange presentiments about clouds and darkness. Lamorna is the cause of all that! ' Eliza smiled comfortingly at her daughter.

'Nathaniel is as sensible as you are, Caroline. It is just that he and Lamorna are obviously very interested in art and that has brought them together. Your father will speak to him and find out what he intends to do, so do not worry.' Caroline looked unconvinced.

Barnabas and Miss Selena did not return for lunch and a disgruntled Austol was forced to return to the Manor. Eliza felt completely overwhelmed by all the conflicting emotions that had been swirling round Roscarne and took refuge in her usual little room at the top of the house. Seated in her chair by the window she looked out at a sky swept clear by the scouring wind and a sea restless with white capped waves. Seth – no, she would not think of Seth. Thoughts of him hurt too much at times. Barnabas? What was his involvement with Miss Selena? Surely he should have found her employment by now and settled her somewhere else? Then there was Austol.

He was not only tiresome but dangerous. Her efforts to help him and the girls seemed to have made him possessive of her. She felt he was trying to tie her to him with bonds of need and indebtedness even in face of her position as a married woman with children. There was more to it than basic attraction, she was sure of that. There were many pretty girls, daughters of aristocratic houses who would serve so well as his wife. Why did he pick on her? Then there was the problem of Lamorna which had made him so angry – and Caroline so sad. She jumped out of her chair. She was not going to allow him to interfere with her family! She needed to talk to somebody. The answer was obvious. Edgar! She would be able to wheedle Edgar into telling her what she needed to know.

16

Finding Edgar was not so easy. Apparently he was doing a tour of duty on a Revenue cutter and would be away from the Manor for a few days. Eliza, impatient to find him, had suffered a fruitless visit to Austol who had, of course, misunderstood the reason for it, preening himself that at last he was making progress in their relationship. Fortunately Kenwyn was visiting and that diluted the awkwardness of being with Austol, especially as Lamorna had not yet been contacted and her father's temper uncertain as a result.

'I do believe, Papa, that she is only fourteen years old?' probed Kenwyn. He was trying not to look pleased that Lamorna had fallen from grace. Too long he, Kenwyn, had been the less favoured one of the family. His handsome face registered some satisfaction.

'She is very nearly fifteen,' said Austol. 'And quite mature enough to realise that her actions are disgraceful. I feel, however, that Nathaniel, who is two years older, is he not?' He looked for confirmation from Eliza, then went on: 'He is the more culpable of the two. It is not the first time that a young girl has been swayed by a handsome young man to act in a reckless way.'

Kenwyn's expression was cynical 'I remember my sister well. If anyone did the persuading it was she. She is the only one of all the girls who has a strong character and always does what she wants. The others are quite feeble next to her.'

'You are being very unkind about your sisters,' reproved Austol. 'I am sure Mistress Eliza is shocked.' Eliza shook her head.

'Not shocked – just surprised. I thought that you had given permission for Lamorna to look for a school of art in

Newlyn or Penzance. If you remember, we talked about it. I thought she would have jumped at the idea.'
'Maybe. But before I could discuss the matter with her she had left.'
'My husband will be visiting Exeter shortly and intends to enquire for news of them at the school. Someone must know where they have gone.'
'I am pleased to hear it.'
'You may have a letter before then of course,' said Kenwyn, twiddling his thumbs and then added, unwisely, 'At least two of your children have had the spirit to do what they want.'
There was a terrible silence. Then Austol rose, his face like thunder, his lean frame towering over his son. 'For that you can thank your mother. She never knew how to curb her inclinations!' He turned to Eliza with a little bow.' Mistress Eliza, please excuse me. I have business to attend to. Kenwyn will see you out. I hope that when you come again, the conversation will be more conducive to a pleasant afternoon!'
He swept out, taking time to glare at his son.

Kenwyn looked abashed and suddenly younger than his twenty one years. He sat obviously embarrassed by the scene with his father.
'I am so sorry, Mistress Eliza. I have ruined your afternoon.'
'No, no, of course not,' said Eliza, hastily. 'You finish your tea and I will finish mine.'
In silence they sipped their tea then Eliza could not resist saying lightly, 'You do have a penchant for irritating your father, Kenwyn. You almost seem to enjoy making him angry!'
Kenwyn looked rueful. 'Not really. And yet I do feel angry with him for much of the time. He is so overbearing and dictatorial.' A quick glance at Eliza. 'And it is his fault that I never knew my mother.
'But –' began Eliza. 'Eulalia?'

'She was not my mother. Eulalia was Papa's second wife. He was married before.'
Perhaps realising that he had just vouched information that was not general knowledge, he jumped to his feet. 'I should not keep you, Mistress Eliza, or you will not reach home before dark. I do apologise again for my unfortunate remarks.'

On the way home, as Mathey was in taciturn mood, Eliza had time to muse on a strange afternoon. She had not known that Eulalia was Austol's second wife. Perhaps Edgar would tell her more. At least she now had an explanation for Austol and his son being so often on a collision course.

Back at Roscarne she found that Barnabas and Selena had not yet returned – as Ewella informed her with some relish. She went in search of Caroline and found her asleep in an armchair in the morning room. There were tracks of tears still on her face. Poor Caroline! It was inevitable that she and Nathaniel, though twins, would tread separate paths as they grew up, their close friendship suffering conflicting demands from others. If it were true that Nathaniel was indeed passionate about painting, Caroline, with her inability even to draw a straight line, would not be able to keep up with him. And Lamorna? Was it a mutual interest in art that drew them together or a mutual attraction? Eliza sighed. So many growing affairs of the heart were fraught with attendant difficulties which tainted the blooms of joy as frosts marred the petals of the rose. And poor Kenwyn. Perpetually angry and unable to resolve it with a father such as Austol, a father without real empathy for a son born of the wrong mother.

The early winter dusk had fallen and Ewella bustled in to light the oil lamps.
'I hope Mr. Barnabas will be back soon. It is nearly suppertime.'
'We can wait a little while, Ewella, I am sure he will not be long,' smiled Eliza, determined not to show her

101

concern. 'I shall go up and see Grace.' Her sister was pacing slowly up and down her room, elegant in a sweeping lilac dress. She greeted Eliza coolly, as a distant acquaintance rather than a sister.

'Richard and Elestren have not been to see me,' she complained. 'And Selena is nowhere to be found. She must do my hair before I can come down to supper.' As an apparent afterthought she asked 'Will that nice Seth Quinn be joining us?'

'Oh yes – and Rose as well.' This did not please Grace who scowled.

'I cannot come down with my hair like this!'

'Shall I do it for you?' offered Eliza. Grace stared at her.

'You?'

'If you will let me.'

Eliza began to brush Grace's hair gently and then became busy with pins and combs. The result was pleasing if not up to Selena's standard and Grace seemed quite appreciative.

'If you ever leave Roscarne I am sure you could earn money as a lady's maid,' she said in condescending tones. Eliza sighed. But at least her sister seemed to know who she was and where she was. Seth would have to look out for himself. Barnabas and Selena did not return in time for supper which made Uncle Tobias voice his disgruntled feelings in no uncertain fashion.

'Mr. Edgar is waiting for you,' said Ewella, the following day, when Eliza returned   after a visit to Rosmorren. 'He looks right handsome in his uniform.' Indeed he did. Eliza was relieved to see that at last he had lost the look of strain he had carried round for so long since that dreadful time at Carnglaze when apparently he had been 'possessed' by the spirit of Samuel Hooper. He seemed much more robust and stood tall, his head straight and his eyes candid.

'I am pleased to see you, Mistress Eliza,' he said as they took tea together. 'I am so sorry if I seemed out of touch with what has been happening at Roscarne – and the Manor, of course.'

'You needed time to recover,' Eliza soothed him.

'I am here to ask for your help again,' he confessed. 'Austol is stamping about the Manor like a tiger whose tail has been trodden on. The girls keep out of his way but the staff is having a difficult time.'

'Lamorna I suppose?'

'Lamorna and Nathaniel!'

'I believe Barnabas is going to visit Exeter to see Nathaniel but I do not know when. For all I know he may have been there already.'

Edgar raised his eyebrows. So Mistress Eliza did not know the whereabouts of her husband.

'Austol, too, has announced his intention of visiting Nathaniel's school,' said Edgar. 'He says he has business in Exeter and will be away for several days – but I am worried for those little girls left in the care of maids. Would it be presuming too much to ask you to visit, just to reassure them? Lamorna, of course, is not there. I have to complete my tour of duty and so am unable to be there. Eliza nodded. Why not? Her own children had Ewella and Rose to look after them and Barnabas was not at home to require her presence.

'Did you ever meet Austol's first wife?' asked Eliza when they were bowling along to the Manor. Edgar looked surprised.

'Very briefly.' He said no more, his lips clamped shut. Eliza realised that she had shown unforgivable curiosity and began chattering about other subjects. Of course Edgar, the brother of Eulalia, would not want to talk about Austol's first wife. Nevertheless she was interested. What had happened? Did she die? Why had Austol never mentioned her?

'The girls will be in the schoolroom,' Edgar volunteered. 'And of course you will stay for supper? I did mention to Ewella that you were unlikely to return to Roscarne before nightfall.'

Austol's girls were little no longer, Eliza thought as they greeted her. They seemed to fill the schoolroom to overflowing. Melwyn, in the absence of Lamorna, was the eldest, a hefty thirteen year old with a wide smile. Kerra, the mischievous one, Eliza remembered, at eleven was growing like a dandelion, her dimity dress barely covering her knees. Elowen, on the other hand seemed unchanged, small with almost white hair and lashes and a shy smile. The triplets, Cryda, Tegen and Caja were already taller than Elowen although a year younger. All those girls! Poor Eulalia! And under pressure from Austol to produce a boy. Another boy. No wonder her health had failed her. No wonder Edgar was concerned about his nieces when Austol seemed preoccupied with business problems, just like Barnabas, and there was the defiance of Lamorna, the eldest girl which Austol had not settled.

At last the girls were all settled in bed; they had tidied up, washed, cleaned their teeth and now looked at Eliza expectantly.
'Will you be here in the morning, Mistress Eliza?'
'No, but I shall come to see you again soon.'
A pause and then Kerra piped up, 'Do you know any stories, Mistress Eliza?'
Eliza looked around the room but there were no books on the shelves. Melwyn informed her that all their books were in the schoolroom as they were not allowed to read at bedtime.
'Papa says we should go to sleep straight away, but that is not always possible.'
Eliza smiled sympathetically.
'Well, I shall start to tell you a story. It is about a girl called Anne and someone else wrote about her but you will

have to put up with my version.' Happily they slid further down their beds and waited.

'This is about a little girl who became an orphan when her parents were killed in an accident. As she had no other relations she was put in an orphanage where she was quite happy – but what she wanted most of all was a family of her own.' She looked around her, wondering if perhaps she had picked on the wrong story. But their eyes were fixed on her as she stumbled through her own much shortened version of Anne of Green Gables. She had reached the point where Anne was being teased in school about her red hair when she realised that her audience were all asleep.

'A success then!' she chuckled to herself and blew out the candles.

17

The next morning Eliza was surprised to meet Edgar at breakfast.

'Is your tour of duty completed then?'

'Oh yes – and successfully! We searched a fishing boat and found it crammed to the gunwales with good French brandy! I have some for Jean Luc' – here Eliza tried not to look disapproving – 'so we should aim for another visit soon. Now, as Austol is not yet returned, I have something you must see.'

'I should leave for Roscarne as soon as possible – Barnabas may be back!' said Eliza.

'This won't take long. Follow me.' And she had perforce to follow him up to the attic room where Austol stored his paintings.

'I know where the key is kept,' whispered Edgar.

'Surely we should wait for Austol's permission?' she protested but Edgar was determined After a brief search he pulled out one of the canvases stacked against the wall and held it up in the best light for Eliza to see. It was the portrait of a woman – an attractive woman with thick dark hair and long lashed dark eyes, a beautiful face but defiant in expression. Her creamy skin was enhanced by a necklace of turquoise stones. She stared out of the portrait with a hauteur that rather detracted from her beauty. Not a willing sitter – but there was something about her –

'Do you not see?' demanded Edgar, with excitement in his voice.

'See what, exactly?'

'When I first saw it I thought it was vaguely familiar! It could be you!'

'Surely not!' said Eliza, shocked. 'She is a beauty! And see, her nose is more definite than mine. Furthermore I hope I would never look quite so disagreeable!'

'Close your eyes!' commanded Edgar. 'Then open them and look again.' Eliza did so.

'Well, yes,' she said cautiously. 'There is a resemblance. Who is she?'

'Jenifer, Austol's first wife!'

On the way back to Roscarne, Eliza remained deep in thought. Tactfully, Edgar remained quiet and concentrated on guiding the pony. Perhaps he should not have shown her the portrait.

'Mr. Barnabas is back,' announced Ewella. 'He is having a late breakfast with Miss Selena in the morning room.' Her voice betrayed nothing of her feelings but she glanced anxiously at her mistress. Things were not as they should be. Her brother was spending time with an unrelated female, whose origins were not known to the rest of the family and his wife seemed to visit Treloyhan Manor rather often – what was going on? Eliza, however, was still immersed in her own thoughts.

'I shall talk to Barnabas later,' she declared.

'So you see, Rose, this does explain why Austol is so interested in me. He must find the similarity reminds him of Jenifer!' Rose looked uneasy.

'I spoke to Kenwyn earlier,' she said, slowly. 'And I received the impression that Austol was extremely angry with his first wife – and as she ran away, her poor son has been at the receiving end of his temper. Take care Eliza, he is a volatile man and we have seen how he can lash out. Remember how he punched Edgar!'

'He was drunk when he did that. At least he always treats me with the utmost courtesy, even though I do not welcome his attentions.' Eliza found herself in the unusual position of defending Austol. After all, he had shown her kindness during their difficult time at Carnglaze, when she had been faced with the double problems of a shortage of money and unquiet spirits in the house.

'I admit that he does make me feel very uncomfortable at times,' she said.

At that moment Richard, Elestren and Joel were shepherded into the room by Grace, of all people. 'Mama, we are going for a walk with Aunt Grace,' cried Joel excitedly. 'We are going up on the moor – '

'And we may find Rosmorren Quoit if we can walk that far!' put in Richard. 'We may go, may we not, Mistress Eliza?' Eliza hesitated. Was it safe to allow Grace out with the children? Her hesitation was noted by her sister who shrugged her shoulders.

'Come with us, Eliza,' she said surprisingly. 'Then your mind will be at rest. The fresh air will do you good. You look terrible. If your visits to Treloyhan Manor cause you such worry you should not go. Austol is able to manage his own concerns without you.'

Eliza gazed at Grace in astonishment. An invitation AND advice from her sister, the most coherent and amiable remarks for some time. As amiable as Grace could manage. That made up her mind.

'Thank you, Grace,' she replied. 'I should love to come.'

'Ewella has made us a picnic,' confided Richard ,

'And we shall open it as soon as we reach the Quoit.'

'What is a quoit?' asked Rose, joining the group.

'A pile of rocks high up on the moor!' chirped Joel.

'More than that!' exclaimed Richard, his face serious with ten year old gravity. 'The stones mark where there is a tomb – Miss Maisie said so!'

'A tomb! A place where they put bodies!' Joel sounded gleeful.

'I do not know if we shall reach it,' said Eliza, hastily. 'It might be rather far for Elestren.'

'I shall take Elestren for you,' interrupted Rose. 'Seth is away at the mine and I am helping Nessa with her reading. We can read stories together.'

'That is very kind of you,' said Grace, again surprising Eliza with her lucidity. Rose held out her hand to Elestren and the little girl toddled off with her quite happily.

'When shall we have our picnic?' demanded Joel.

'As soon as we feel hungry.'

'I am hungry now!' announced Joel. At this point, Miss Maisie click-clacked into the room.

'There you are!' she exclaimed. 'Have you forgotten it is a school day? I have been waiting for you in the schoolroom.'

'We are going on a walk,' explained Richard. 'I thought you knew.' He looked quite upset that they might have offended their teacher. For a ten year old, he was unusually aware of other people's feelings, a trait Eliza had noticed before.

'Oh, it is my fault. I should have told you,' said Grace, airily.

'We are going to see Rosmorren Quoit,' Richard added. Miss Maisie's face lit up.

'May I accompany you?' she asked excitedly. 'I so love quoits and standing stones...!'

'Of course. But you need to change your shoes!' smiled Eliza, looking at Miss Maisie's neat button boots. Grace looked uncertain. Her walk was becoming crowded.

The climb up to Rosmorren Moor was deceptively steep and the rusty coloured bracken scratchy so they were all relieved to reach the place where the ground levelled off and they could pause and look around. In the distance, the sea looked still as a painting, calm in spite of the continual wind which blustered around them; the fields were green pieces of jigsaw separated by granite walls, the cattle like wooden toys. And scattered into the distance over the moor, tall chimneys marked the position of tin mines.

'We have walked a long way!' said Grace. 'In spite of the wind I feel quite warm.'

'So do I!' cried Joel, capering round. 'Can we have our picnic now?' Grace and Eliza laughed at the same time and Eliza had the warm feeling that perhaps they were actually together on this jaunt.

Meanwhile Miss Maisie was stepping daintily along trying to avoid catching her long skirts on the grasping bracken. The picnic was not lavish as Ewella had been unaware of the enlarged group. In any case she was scornful of winter picnics, considering them risky as the weather could be uncertain and change in a trice. But the little party fell on the food with appreciation and even Grace, her appetite always picky, enjoyed a large saffron bun.

After they had eaten every crumb and crunched every apple, Grace fell asleep with startling suddenness. Richard moved closer to his beloved Eliza, hoping she would chat to him, something his mother never did. That left Joel still full of energy and desperate to continue the walk. Miss Maisie rose to the occasion.

'Perhaps Joel and I could walk ahead? We shall keep to this path and then you can catch up when you are ready.'

'I expect Grace will wake up soon,' said Eliza.

Happily, Joel skipped along next to Miss Maisie while Grace slept on, her face peaceful, her fair hair ruffled in the wind. Eliza and Richard waited patiently. Then something made Eliza sit up straight.

'What was that!' she demanded. It came again, a thin scream, quavery and distorted by the gusts of wind.

'It sounds like Miss Maisie!' said Richard. 'Perhaps there's been an accident!' Eliza scrambled to her feet, her face white. She shook her sister awake.

'Grace, will you wait for us here? I must go and see what has happened.'

'I shall come with you,' declared Richard. Eliza wasted no time in arguing but set off at a run across the tussocky grass. Her vision ahead was impeded by a rise in the terrain which slowed her down and made her breathe heavily. Surmounting this was not the end of it. Ahead lay a steep decline and then another climb. No sign of Joel and Miss Maisie and no more screams.

'We had better stick to the path,' panted Eliza, as Richard caught up with her. 'Surely they cannot be much further ahead.' They toiled up the next incline.

'Look at that!' exclaimed Richard. 'It's a derelict mine.' A tumble of buildings lay ahead. 'See, some of the buildings are broken down – and there are creepers growing into the windows.' As he spoke there was another scream. It was Miss Maisie without a doubt and she sounded terrified.

'Over here! Over here!' Her voice seemed to be coming from a rough area littered with rocks and covered with bramble bushes not far from the base of the engine house. The chimney stood as if on guard over the crumbling building –and as a sentinel of warning. The idea of approaching such a place did not appeal. Eliza put her hand on Richard's arm.

'We must take care – where there are mine buildings there are shafts – deep shafts, so please follow me, Richard.' Cautiously she approached the mine, awed by the vastness of the buildings and the menace of the chimney at close quarters. Then she stopped. Miss Maisie's voice came from her feet.

'Here – we are here! Mind where you step!' There was fear in her voice. 'Joel is holding on to me or I would have fallen.'

Eliza peered through the brambles and was horrified to see how they masked a large black hole. She shivered. The mine was like a creature waiting to trap its prey, she thought. And it had trapped Miss Maisie and Joel. She could just discern Miss Maisie's white face turned upwards and behind her, Joel.

'I can't move!' her voice was muted with terror. 'I'm on a ledge and Joel has hold of my arm and if he lets go I shall fall – I know I shall fall! Please help us!' She sounds near to hysteria, Eliza thought, horror stricken herself at the thought of the governess flailing around in terror and causing both of them to fall. Then Joel's voice.

'We need a rope, Mama, and then we can hold on to it while you pull us out.' His voice was calm. 'We are not far down but there is nothing to hold on to.' A rope! Eliza thought frantically. Was she expected to find a rope lying about on this bleak moorland? Where would she get a rope? Eventually, with two of her petticoats and Richard's shirt, she manufactured a rope strong enough, she hoped, to hold their weight. It did and soon Miss Maisie, gasping like a fish, was lying on the grass. Joel hauled himself up with speed and fell into his mother's arms.

'I was all right, Mama, but Miss Maisie has vert … verti … – she is terrified of heights! And that shaft was deep. I dropped a stone down it and could not hear when it hit the bottom!'

'Joel is a hero!' sobbed Miss Maisie. 'He held on to me all that time and saved me!'

18

Barnabas was not pleased. In fact, when he heard the full story of Grace's ill-fated walk, he was furious.

'Eliza, the irresponsibility you showed is beyond a joke. Allowing Grace – Grace of all people to arrange such an outing! Then permitting Miss Maisie to take Joel out of sight on such uncertain terrain! What were you thinking about!'

'I was enjoying the fact that Grace was able to suggest such a walk!' retorted Eliza. 'She has rarely shown any interest in accompanying the children anywhere – and she invited me, which I took as a compliment.' She hesitated to go on, intimidated by the rage in Barnabas' face.

'And Miss Maisie? Apparently it was a school day and she and the children should have been doing schoolwork, not rambling over the moors!'

'It was a historical ramble!' insisted Eliza. 'We were going to look at Rosmorren Quoit but it was further than we thought.' Even to her own ears that sounded feeble.

'And were you not aware of the dangers posed by derelict mines and unguarded shafts? You, a tin miner's daughter?'

'I am now!' said Eliza bitterly. Then her own rage bubbled up. 'Perhaps if the children's father showed more interest in them rather than spending all his spare time with a stray female we might have received the benefit of his advice! Furthermore,' Eliza went on, feeling that she might just as well be hung for a sheep as a lamb, 'I should like to have a private talk with you, Barnabas! We have things to discuss.' Barnabas glared at his wife and then strode out of the room, colliding with Ewella in the doorway.

'Did you hear how brave Joel was?' Ewella demanded. 'He saved Miss Maisie and she cannot stop talking about it!' If she hoped to lighten her brother's mood it did not work.

'He gets angry so easily these days,' Eliza complained. Rose looked up from the book she was reading to Elestren.

'Trouble at Wheal Eliza?' she suggested. 'Or at one of the other mines? You know how upset he gets if anything goes wrong.'

'He has not been there this week. He seems to have been taking Selena here, there and everywhere. Rosmorren, Falmouth, Truro ....'

'Then perhaps it is Nathaniel and Lamorna and their rebellious determination to keep painting?' Rose was uneasy about discussing Barnabas and Selena. She, too, could not understand Barnabas' apparent obsession with the girl.

'I am going to tackle him on the subject,' said Eliza, darkly.

Eliza faced her husband in his study. It was a handsome room, though too dark and cluttered with furniture for her taste. Barnabas sat at his vast mahogany desk and looked enquiring, his temper outburst forgotten it seemed. However she still felt that she was being treated as a delinquent.

'What did you want to talk to me about, Eliza?' he asked.

'I should like to sit down,' said his wife coldly. 'What I wish to say will take more than a few minutes.' Her husband jumped up to hold a chair for her, muttering apologies. Eliza sat straight backed, her face devoid of expression.

'I want to know more about Selena. Why is she here? I understood it was only to be for a short time. Then why are you spending so much time with her? You seem to have no time for the children, for Uncle Tobias or – or me!' At this point her voice cracked. Barnabas looked briefly startled, then uncomfortable.

'Selena's father was in prison with me,' he began, slowly. 'He was a good friend to me and I would not have survived that place without him. My sentence was quashed, as I told you, but he had a much longer time to serve.' Eliza's lip curled at this. 'I promised to go to Falmouth where his wife and daughter were living and find out how they were – which I did. It was there I succumbed to influenza and his wife nursed me back to health. I was very low at that time – the hardships of the places I worked and then the shock of a false accusation and imprisonment had already reduced me from the man I was.' He leaned forward and looked sternly at Eliza. 'You must understand that it was the kindness of Selena and her mother that restored me. Furthermore, she introduced me to the owner of several tin mines in the Camborne area. We worked well together and, to cut a long story short, when we found substantial new lodes we both made money.

Eliza remained silent, drawn in to this story against her will. Barnabas poured himself a glass of brandy and drank it down at one gulp.

'When I realised I was fit enough and wealthy enough I knew I could come home. But – a letter arrived announcing the death of Selena's father in prison. Of course, she and her mother were distraught and I had to stay and sort out their affairs, which delayed me still more. Eventually the mother settled down and Selena obtained employment in a hairdressing salon and seemed more resigned to what had happened. So I came home.'

Eliza had regained her composure but her lovely eyes were glacial as she regarded her husband.

'Why did you not send me a letter? Did you not realise that we were all so worried about you? We had not heard from you for so long! And I was struggling with all the children, Uncle Tobias AND Grace in a house that was not only derelict but HAUNTED?'

'I did not realise that, certainly. But you must understand that I could not come home to you penniless and broken down in health?' There was pleading in his voice that Eliza chose to ignore.

'Pride!' she spat. 'Just masculine pride! I could have nursed you and at least I would have had some support in that dreadful house! 'And now – why is Selena here? I am sorry her mother died but – '

'I promised my friend I would take care of her – and her mother,' said Barnabas, obstinacy in his tone. A nerve was twitching just above his eye, a sign of stress that Eliza recognised.

'Admirable, I am sure. But there are limits. Selena is not really employed here. Grace has dispensed with her services and Rose seems to have taken over. Surely Selena could seek a post elsewhere and make a new life of her own?'

'You have no idea how difficult she is!' retorted Barnabas. 'If I mention that very same idea to her she becomes extremely upset. I feel she still needs my help and I am working on it. I shall find the solution to her neediness soon. While we are on the subject, why is it that Austol needs so much help – and from you?'

'He is a friend and relation and turns to us because of that.'

'And I have not complained.'

'It is not the same situation!' flared Eliza, her heart sinking as she recognised that there were similarities. At this point, the door burst open and in came Joel, his blue eyes shining and, as usual, his red hair standing up like a cockerel's.

'I have written about my adventure like a story!' he announced. 'And Miss Maisie says I should call it 'The Hero'! His father and mother could only look at him proudly though both knew he needed a reprimand for his unorthodox entry.

'And I have learned a new word! Miss Maisie has vertigo which makes her dizzy near heights, It was lucky I was there to hold her hand!' There was no disputing this.

Uncle Tobias was her next port of call. He had the power to soothe her indignant feelings without actually saying anything and the two of them could sit together and chat gently, leaving both feeling calmed. Eliza knew that Uncle Tobias did have a view of the Selena situation but felt that it was not his business to intervene.

'Barnabas has his reasons,' was all he would say. 'He has more sense than you credit him with, Eliza my dear and you will find that things will work out in the fullness of time. Now, how about a little of my best brandy?'

19

It was Uncle Tobias who voiced a thought that had already occurred to Eliza.

'That Selena, she looks like the cat that's had the cream,' he muttered as he took his place for supper that night. Indeed Selena did not look like the same girl who had appeared on the doorstep of Roscarne. Then she had been shabbily dressed and so shy she could not look at anyone, a poor creature without home or relations. Now Eliza observed her as she came in to the dining room just behind Barnabas. She was wearing a new dress of ruched taffeta with a tight bodice ornamented with beads which caught the light and her thick black hair was tamed, upswept and elegant. It was her demeanour, however, which was remarkably different. She held her head high and her glance was almost arrogant as she looked round the assembled family, eyes glittering in her pale face. Kind Rose leaned towards her and complimented her on the dress, eliciting a slight smile.

'Such a pretty brooch?' probed Ewella.

'Left to me by my mother,' replied Selena, complacently. Her long fingers touched the oval of gold inset with a cabochon garnet surrounded by amethysts. There was no doubting the quality of the jewel, nor the expense of her new dress; together they presented an entirely new Selena.

'No wonder she looks so pleased with herself,' muttered Ewella.

Barnabas did not heed this exchange. He and Seth were deep in discussion about Wheal Rose and no one dared to interrupt them. Eliza was puzzled. Selena had arrived on the doorstep of Roscarne with all she possessed in a threadbare woven bag of no great size. How had she acquired the dress – there was no room in the bag and she was apparently penniless. Certainly the occasional tasks she undertook in the house would not pay enough to allow such a purchase? Eliza resolved to question Barnabas on the subject as, of course, all remuneration was dealt out by the master of Roscarne.

'It is time I went shopping to Truro,' declared Grace, breaking the sudden silence as Barnabas and Seth completed their discussion. Everyone turned to look at her as her contributions to the general talk were infrequent. 'If Selena has a new dress so should I. Barnabas,' she appealed to her brother-in-law. 'I do not have enough money. I need a new dress.' Barnabas looked severe.

'Grace, you have your own money and you do have enough!' he said. 'We are happy to have you here as our guest but I am not able to fund your wardrobe as well.'

'You buy Selena clothes. And she is not even family,' said Grace sulkily. Her eyes were filling with tears and Eliza could sense a tantrum was building which could be as damaging as any tropical storm.

'This is not a suitable subject for the supper table,' she said hurriedly. 'Grace, you and I will talk afterwards.' Grace subsided and a momentary look of triumph flashed across Selena's face.

Discussions about shopping and new dresses took second place when another unwelcome piece of news was delivered by Edgar, who arrived after breakfast the next day.

'I am the bearer of bad tidings,' he said portentously. 'Austol would have come himself but he is bedridden with a bad attack of gout. 'I am afraid that Lamorna and Nathaniel have run away to London.' This was greeted with a stricken silence. Then everyone started talking at once.

'I went to see Nathaniel at school in Exeter!' said Barnabas, his face white. 'He told me that he was buckling down to his exams and would be home in a few weeks. He said nothing about Lamorna!'

'Is it certain that they went to London?' asked Eliza, without much hope.

'They left a brief note for Austol and said that they would be writing to you.' Edgar would not meet her eyes. He had known something like this was brewing.

'Why did the school not inform me?' thundered Barnabas, rage taking over from dismay.

'Perhaps you could see Austol to talk about it,' muttered Edgar. 'He will have made enquiries and would be most relieved to see you.' Seth had ushered Rose away, feeling this was none of their business but Ewella and Grace were exclaiming and twittering like birds. Fortunately the children were in the schoolroom with Miss Maisie and Uncle Tobias had already retired to his study but even so the bad news crackled round the house as speedily as a moorland blaze.

'Such a good-looking young man,' said Mrs. Adwyn, sadly. 'It always seems to be the good-looking ones who lead the girls astray.'

'Not always. That Lamorna be a 'ansome looking girl,' chimed in Suki, a housemaid. 'She do seem to be stronger than Master Nathaniel, more bossy like.'

'Come with me, Eliza,' said Barnabas tersely. 'We shall go to see Austol. He will have to get out of his bed to discuss this little matter with us!' They drove in silence to the Manor and waited in the drawing room for Austol to put in an appearance. Eliza was shocked to see how haggard he looked when he did come.

'This is a bad business,' he said, shaking his head. 'I knew Lamorna was keen to go to Art School but I thought she was resigned to a school in Newlyn or Penzance. And to go with Nathaniel!' He looked reproachfully at Eliza.

'They have been friends for a long time, apparently,' was all she could manage.

'But Nathaniel is not as interested in painting as your girl!' interrupted Barnabas. 'He has clearly been pushed in that direction!'

'Your son has taken Lamorna, an under-age girl, to London. Where will they live? What are they doing for money? Austol was beside himself. Barnabas could find nothing to say.

It was Eliza who had some sensible suggestions.

'Perhaps we could ask Aunt Gloria to help in tracking them down,' she said. 'Though it might be too much of a burden for an old lady. Or we could ask Jean Luc if he has any ideas.'

'Jean Luc?' queried Barnabas.

'A friend of Edgar's – he is a painter and has a gallery in Newlyn.'

'How do you know all this?' Barnabas' voice had grown dangerously soft.

'I shall tell you on the way back. Of course you have been too involved in mining business to keep up with what has been happening to your children.' Eliza could not resist the barb. She hoped that her husband would not give her the sharp answer she expected in front of Austol. But it was true. The mines were of utmost importance to Barnabas and he relied on her to manage house, children, relations and staff. She even had to remind him to spend time with Uncle Tobias.

On the way back, a morose Barnabas listened, in growing disbelief, how his wife and Edgar had visited Jean Luc in Newlyn.

'You never told me,' he reproached. 'And your trip was hardly proper! Anyone could have seen you!'

'You were not around at the time,' Eliza said, determined to keep her temper. 'And I feel that if it was proper for me to go to St. Michael's Mount with Seth it was certainly proper to go with Edgar on a visit to discover what was happening with Nathaniel. Besides which, I am NOT a young girl and I do what I consider appropriate!' Barnabas grunted. Eliza swept on 'And you went to Exeter and allowed that headmaster to sway you with unctuous words while Nathaniel was clearly out of control, taking time to visit Newlyn without his knowledge.'

'As Selena pointed out to me, YOU are out of control!' snapped Barnabas. 'She said that no wife of her acquaintance would behave as you do – and I agree with her!'

Eliza could hardly believe her ears.

'You have discussed me with Selena! How dare you! And how dare she pass judgment on me! And obviously you did not defend me, my dear husband! But perhaps I should remind you that I am a person in my own right, not a young girl. Sometimes you treat me like a child in the schoolroom.' Hurt and anger vied in her voice. The rest of the journey was silent.

20

A visit to Jean Luc was not productive. Faced with an angry Barnabas he retreated into such broken English that he conveyed very little information of use. Yes, he had seen Lamorna and Nathaniel briefly and had been impressed by their enthusiasm for painting but knew nothing more. Neither did he offer his visitor a glass of his good brandy.

'Un couple tres gentil,' he said to Edgar who also came visiting later. 'It ees so sad to 'ave such a father, so angry and not –not raisonnable!'

'Do you know where they are?' pressed Edgar.

'Non.'

Eliza went to confide in her dear friend Rose. Her conscience was troubling her after her day with Seth but Rose was her usual sunny self.

'Seth and Barnabas have gone to Wheal Rose,' she said. 'That leaves us free for a good chat.'

Eliza gave her a wan smile. She related her conversation with Barnabas and was comforted by her friend's indignation on her behalf.

'I cannot believe that Barnabas is stupid enough to confide in Selena! She is nearly young enough to be his daughter!'

'Neither can I believe that he would betray me in such a way,' said Eliza, helplessly. 'Yet he spends so much time with her and she is always hanging on to every word he says. I admit I am jealous!'

'You must insist that she is sent out to find employment,' said Rose. 'Such a situation can only develop if it is allowed to continue. You are Barnabas' wife and you have a right to make such a demand. Uncle Tobias thinks she should leave Roscarne and find somewhere else to live!'

Days passed and nothing changed. Austol was still suffering a bad attack of gout which immobilized him and though Barnabas journeyed yet again to Exeter and then to Newlyn he was unable to find any trace of the delinquent pair. Selena, meanwhile, had obviously decided to improve herself in various ways. She arranged and rearranged the flowers which arrived from Austol's hot house so regularly and thumped on the piano in the morning room. She was seen sewing assiduously and embroidering various cushion covers with growing skill. All this took her away from the duties expected of her and no complaints from Grace made any difference, neither did the sharp remonstrances from Ewella have any effect. Eliza decided to ignore what was happening – Selena was in the household because Barnabas wished it and there was no more to be said. She was certainly not going to involve herself in any fracas with the newcomer, that interloper, she thought bitterly. No. A dignified withdrawal was her intention.

Eliza was in the schoolroom with Miss Maisie who had been more nervous and jumpy than usual and welcomed some help. It seemed that her near fall down the mineshaft at Rosmorren Quoit had shaken her more than she admitted. In the midst of a history lesson, the door opened quietly. Nathaniel stood there.

'Nathaniel – oh Nathaniel!' was all Eliza could manage. Caroline left her seat and rushed to hug her brother while the others looked on, big eyed.

'Come – come to the morning room and you must tell me what has happened. Miss Maisie will continue with the lesson and you shall all see Nathaniel later.' She beckoned her eldest son who followed her.

MARAH COVE

Once in the morning room he sat in an armchair and put his head in his hands, alarming his mother.

'Nathaniel, what has happened? Where have you been? Where are Lamorna and John?' She could not stop the flow of questions and felt that she was babbling like a stream over pebbles. 'Let me look at you! It seems so long since I saw you!'

Nathaniel looked up at her and his face was that of a young man, not the boy who had gone away to school. He looked gaunt and his eyes were shadowed.

'John is still at school. Lamorna has returned to the Manor. We are not together anymore.' He spoke flatly but his expression betrayed his anguish.

'I think you need some refreshment before you tell me anymore,' said Eliza. Her son was no longer a boy but a young man, suffering a young man's sorrow. She must bolster his spirits before Barnabas returned and began to scold him, a scolding which would, in all probability, make matters worse. Fortified with tea and a saffron bun, Nathaniel talked briefly to his mother.

'I am sorry to have caused you distress, Mama,' he muttered. 'I know you will feel let down because I have not finished school nor taken my exams. I felt that what I was doing was more important for shaping my life and I knew that Papa would not agree with my actions. So I am back and I shall do as you and he suggest, whether it be to return to school or stay and find employment.'

'Your painting? Are you serious about it?'

'Totally. I shall continue in my spare time. If I get any! But I am conscious that I have behaved badly.'

Eliza gazed at him, taking care to avoid censure in her look.

'And Lamorna?' she asked quietly.

'I should prefer not to talk about her.' Like a trap his mouth snapped shut. He went up to his room and there he stayed for the rest of the day.

Barnabas did not return till late in the day and it took all Eliza's powers of persuasion to prevent him from stamping upstairs to confront their son.

'He will be fast asleep by now – he looked absolutely exhausted. And you will be calmer after a good night's rest and then you can listen to his explanations in a reasonable frame of mind.'

'Are you suggesting I am not reasonable?'

'I know that you are late and tired and I don't suppose you have had any supper. I shall bring you a plate of squab pie and something to drink before you retire.'

'Thank you, Eliza. Your diplomacy could have prevented the Transvaal War! Now where is Selena?' Always Selena! Eliza could have screamed. But she did not.

'Selena is in the drawing room, embroidering I believe.' She spoke in cool tones.

'Not the best use of her time, I should imagine.' said her husband. 'Is she still doing Grace's hair? And has she listened to instructions from Ewella on how to deport herself as a lady's maid?'

'You had better ask her,' replied a surprised Eliza. She left the room but a screech from Selena stopped her in her tracks. Despising herself for listening, she crept closer to the half open door. There was the rumble of Barnabas' voice and then, very clearly, the answer from Selena.

'I am tired of looking! I want to stay here – and no, not as a lady's maid! I want to be a member of your family. Just you remember how well we treated you and how my mother looked after you!' Then came the answer from Barnabas, so low that Eliza had to strain to hear.

'Selena, be reasonable. Of course you can stay here while we are looking but I cannot just adopt you into the family!'

Barnabas pushed back his chair and stood up. Eliza crept away, unwilling to be caught in such a demeaning position. But she was even more puzzled. What were they looking for? A place of employment for Selena? And why would a young girl like Selena want to belong to their family? Was it because of Barnabas? Was she in love with Barnabas? And was her husband trying to wriggle out of a difficult situation? Should she ask him? Then she would have to admit that she had been eavesdropping. That was out of the question.

A shock awaited them all the next day. Austol, driven by Edgar, turned up before the sun had appeared over the high moor. Clearly suffering, he walked with the aid of a silver handled ebony cane with which he rapped on the door. A startled Ewella showed him into the morning room and hurried to fetch her brother. That Austol was angry was not in doubt. Barnabas found him limping up and down his face a mask of fury.

    'Where is she? I understood that they were both returning home! They have not appeared and I want to know where they are and what they are up to now!'

21

'We quarrelled,' said Nathaniel, miserably. 'She said she did not want to see me again and she would find her own way back to the Manor.'

'And you let her!' Austol was incredulous.

'She had a friend who had promised to take her. One of the reasons why we – we were not getting on.'

'A man friend I take it?'

'Yes.'

'Where were you staying before?' Austol homed in, relentlessly.

'With that friend. He had an apartment.'

'Now do you understand why I feel that Lamorna is too young to be in London! If this story gets out, her reputation will be in shreds! Now, what is this friend's name and I need to know the address.'

'I have nothing else to say.' The young man was white but determined. He did not turn his head as his father came in. Austol nodded curtly and continued in scolding tone.

'We shall see about that! Barnabas, please discipline your son! He ran away with my daughter and now he will not help me to find her!'

'Nathaniel!' exclaimed Barnabas. 'Lord Treloyhan has a right to any information you have.'

'I gave Lamorna my word.' More Nathaniel would not say, however furiously Barnabas and Austol raved at him. Then Eliza intervened. She was alarmed at the expression on her son's face and felt that the cross questioning had gone on long enough.

'Surely Lamorna will have returned to the Manor by now if this – this friend was bringing her back. Perhaps you should return, Austol, and see if that has happened.'

'Oh yes, Papa, she is back. But she would not talk to us and has gone out again with her easel and paints.' This was Melwyn.
'We are so glad she is back,' chorused the triplets. 'You won't be too angry with her, Papa?'
Their father did not answer but his face still looked thunderous.
'Please tell me at once when she returns!' he ordered and limped off to his study. The little girls looked at one another in dismay. Melwyn shrugged. Her father was not in emollient mood. She did not envy poor Lamorna who was obviously going to have to pay for her escapade.

However lunchtime came and went and there was no sign of the errant Lamorna. The early afternoon passed and Austol became more concerned than angry. Edgar was dispatched again to Roscarne to see if they had any news. They had not. A search party was suggested, though Austol would not be able to join them because of his leg.
'She will have found a good place to paint and forgotten the time,' said Nathaniel wearily. 'She will probably be on the cliffs or somewhere on the moor.'

Barnabas forbore to scold his son but sent him off with Edgar to search the Marah cliffs. He himself decided to tackle the moor behind the house, insisting that Eliza should accompany him. Caroline did not wait for permission but scurried after her brother. She would support him whatever happened.

The warmth and light of the day were fading as the two parties set off and Eliza was glad of her merino shawl. Barnabas was uncommunicative as they toiled up the steep slopes, reaching Rosmorren Quoit from where they could see the spread of the countryside around.

'She could be anywhere around here,' said Eliza helplessly. 'We might be able to see a long way but she could be hidden nearby on the other side of one of the ridges.'

Barnabas gave her a brief smile. 'Let's shout, then,' he suggested. Which they did until they were hoarse. No reply, only the indignant fluttering of some birds, disturbed by the unfamiliar noise.

'We shall take this direction,' said Barnabas. The terrain they followed echoed a rough sea in solid form, ridge after ridge hiding the view ahead until the two of them came suddenly on the broken down chimney that Eliza remembered from their ill-fated walk.

'There is nothing here she would want to paint,' said Barnabas in disgust.

'It is quite a dramatic scene – she does not always paint people and pretty things,' replied Eliza. Barnabas looked at her sharply. This was not the first time his wife had displayed opinions rooted in knowledge not available to him. How did she know that? What else did she know about Lamorna and Austol and the Manor?

As the sun was drifting down to touch the sea, growing larger as it neared the horizon and drenching the sky with fiery red, Barnabas decided the two of them should return to Roscarne. Nathaniel, Caroline and Edgar arrived just after them, also admitting failure. Edgar set off for the Manor to report, hoping that Lamorna would have turned up. He was getting tired of the endless trips between Roscarne and the Manor. Meanwhile Seth had returned from Wheal Rose and heard about the search from Ewella.

'It will be dark soon,' he exclaimed. 'Surely the silly girl will have returned home by now!' Ewella was surprised that Seth seemed more worried than annoyed – but then he knew the dangers of the coast far better than she did.

'Mistress Eliza – what does she think?

'She's more worried about Nathaniel.'

'Oh?'

'He has not been himself at all since he came back – very down and depressed.' Ewella warmed to her theme. 'He refused to talk to Barnabas or Lord Treloyhan which made them both angry – very angry – and then Mistress Eliza suggested that Lord Treloyhan should go back to the Manor. Which he did. He always does what she says.' She stopped, suddenly aware that Seth was frowning.

'This is serious. She cannot be left out all night if she has injured herself.'

'I think Mr. Barnabas believes she has gone back to London – caught a coach to Penzance, perhaps and then the train.' Eliza came into the room, drawn by Seth's voice and shook her head.

'I am sure she intended to return to the Manor – then found Austol was not there so she decided to do some painting. Best way to avoid thinking of the scolding she was sure to suffer after running away like that. We know she took her easel and paints after all,' she said.

'Then we should organise one last search this evening,' declared Seth. 'I shall go – I'll just inform Rose.'

'I shall come with you,' said Eliza, steadfastly ignoring his concern for Rose. 'And I shall ask Nathaniel. I believe he might be more helpful if his father is not around.'

Nathaniel joined in the search, though his dour expression was not encouraging.

'We have not looked nearer to home,' Eliza pointed out. 'Marah Cliffs are further along but perhaps she went to Marah Cove.' 'She thinks Marah Cove is a romantic spot,' muttered Nathaniel.

'We shall start there,' said Seth.

The three of them scrambled down the narrow path to the shore. The scar from the cliff fall was clearly visible and the yellow of the sand still glowed in the half light. The incoming tide splashed lazily over the rocks, an un-threatening silver touched indigo, while a luminous sky provided the backdrop. A beautiful scene. But then Nathaniel drew in his breath.

'Look!' Unable to utter another syllable he just pointed. A wooden object was being washed up on the shore. A wave – stronger than some – deposited it on the sand. With a strangled cry, Nathaniel rushed towards it and rescued it from the encroaching waves. It was unmistakeably an easel, with one leg broken off. He held it up, despair written over his face. Eliza put her arms around him while Seth went to climb the nearest high point and gaze out to sea, shouting Lamorna's name. They waited and watched and scrambled over the rocks, Nathaniel screaming for Lamorna, but the incoming tide brought in only clumps of trailing bladderwrack and finally it became too dark to see. It was a disconsolate three who returned to the house to be met by Grace exclaiming that they were so late for supper and she was hungry and did they have no thought for other people, chasing after a feckless girl who was quite old enough to know better.

'I tried to make her go back to her room,' said Ewella, helplessly.' But she would not listen to me or Uncle Tobias. Oh,' she turned to Seth. 'And Mistress Rose has been complaining of another megrim .... ' Muttering an imprecation, Seth hurried off to see to his wife.

Supper that night was a gloomy affair; everyone seemed occupied by thoughts that were not cheerful. Only Grace chattered on in her mindless way, apparently unaware of the tension around her.

Eliza found it difficult to sleep that night. Pictures of rearing waves and sharp pointed rocks kept flashing through her mind, interspersed with gaping holes which, magnet-like, drew her towards their Stygian depths. One particularly horrible nightmare made her moan out loud.

'Eliza? What is the matter?' She had awakened Barnabas. His voice was soft and kinder than usual. When she choked out the reason he gathered her close, stroking her hair.

'I'm sure there will be a sensible explanation for Lamorna's disappearance my dear. Now close your eyes and sleep.' Thus reassured she curled up against her husband, taking comfort in his presence and warmth and fell into a deep dark sleep.

She woke with a start to find Barnabas was getting dressed.

'I shall wander along the shore and check all of Marah Cove,' he said briefly.

'I shall come too.'

They left the house as the early light of day was strengthening – to find that Nathaniel was before them. Their son was down on the sand, by the tideline, on his knees, his narrow frame shaken by great gulping sobs. Before him, her hair spread out like seaweed and her face pale as pearl, was Lamorna. She looked like a sleeping mermaid. But she was dead.

22

The next week was a nightmare. The monstrous gift brought in by the tide shattered the peace of both Roscarne and the Manor. Sometimes Eliza felt that nothing would return to normal. Nathaniel immured himself in his room, grey faced, refusing to talk or eat, while Caroline hovered near his door, talking to him softly and trying to persuade him with little titbits, heartbroken that her twin was suffering so. John came back from school on Eliza's insistence; suddenly her family seemed precarious and she wanted all of them under her eye. John was not really concerned with Lamorna, whom he hardly knew, but had grown up sufficiently to sympathise with his brother. He was quite impressed with the audacious way Nathaniel and Lamorna had escaped both home and school but the terrible outcome proved a salutary lesson. Not that he would run away with any girl but he rather hankered after visits to Exeter or Plymouth or even London. With a sigh he relinquished any such idea; his mother was keeping a firm grasp on her family.

Barnabas no longer raged about the house but loped restlessly from room to room and Eliza could not reach him or cheer him. Seth, meanwhile, visited the mines to see that all was well and was hardly back at Roscarne until late evening while Rose languished in her room, suffering the tyranny of frequent megrims. Richard, Elestren, Nessa and Joel were unusually subdued but Miss Maisie kept them occupied in the schoolroom away from Grace who was going through a bad patch where she was not sure which, if any, of the children were hers. Ewella and Mrs. Adwyn kept to the kitchen while poor Uncle Tobias was sadly neglected, without any convivial company at all. And Selena? She tried to rouse Barnabas from his misery but finally gave up and made Mathey take her on outings in the pony and trap.

Back at the Manor, Edgar reported, Austol was grief stricken but grimly controlling his feelings for the sake of his other daughters. They, on the other hand, were weeping and wailing and inconsolable. The message that Edgar brought included a plea for Eliza to visit as soon as she could to help the girls but of course Austol understood that she had her own son to console.

'Edgar, I am not able to come to the Manor as yet,' Eliza insisted. 'Once the funeral is over and things settle down of course I will come.' She did not confide in Barnabas about this plea from Austol, sensing that it would only anger him. She knew that her husband was already disturbed that Nathaniel was being blamed entirely for the tragedy. Only her sisters and Kenwyn were aware of Lamorna's headstrong nature and the probability that she had instigated the idea of running away. But, as Eliza tried to point out, blame did not change what had happened and could not reverse events. Upon which her husband grunted in agreement though there was more to be said on the whole subject.

The funeral service, conducted by Nicholas Tregadillett in Rosmorren Church, was crowded with local people as well as those from the Manor and Roscarne, a terrifying throng bravely faced by Nathaniel. Austol entered the church, so rigidly controlled he might have been one of the statues in the graveyard. He looked neither to the right or left of him and acknowledged no one. Kenwyn followed, handsome in his uniform and only Edgar, bringing up the rear, looked a touch dishevelled, his clothes badly put together and his black coat creased. Barnabas and Eliza stood together with Seth and Rose, a red-eyed Caroline next to them. Further back, Ewella and Mrs. Adwyn supported each other, having been given special permission by Barnabas to be at the funeral even though it was not usual for domestics to attend.

Later, Nathaniel stood, pale and quiet by the grave as the coffin was lowered into the ground and he stayed there, head bowed while everyone left and the new turf was covered with flowers. Caroline remained with her brother, refusing to leave him. It was Kenwyn who came to stand beside the two of them, ready to escort them to Roscarne when they were ready. His father had refused to host any kind of funeral reception so Eliza and Ewella had taken over and a subdued group gathered in the drawing room at Roscarne. But Nathaniel, Caroline and Kenwyn did not return to Roscarne until everyone had gone and ever curious Morwenna Tregadillett was denied a last glimpse of Nathaniel about whom there had been so much gossip.

Several weeks passed but Eliza could not bring herself to visit the Manor. She busied herself by making a fuss of Uncle Tobias, trying to make up for a week's neglect, then checking with Mrs. Adwyn that menus were varied and interesting in order to tempt so many with poor appetites. In the same way she suggested to Miss Maisie that lessons should be particularly entertaining and engrossing to divert the children's minds. Rose she encouraged to leave her room in spite of her headaches and took her for walks in the fresh air, not down by the sea but towards the moorland. Marah Cove was somewhere she could not yet face. The walks did Rose good. They brought colour to her cheeks and loosened her tongue so that she and Eliza could chat about Nathaniel. It was that thorny subject which brought about a rift with Seth. He came in late one evening, obviously tired and fractious. Eliza fussed round him, making sure he had some supper as dinner was long past then sat down with him over a cup of coffee. Seth admitted it would be good if Barnabas returned to work soon. Alterations were needed at Wheal Rose which required his attention.

'What was Nathaniel thinking of?' he groaned, too tired to be tactful and offering a remark which caused Eliza to stiffen.

'I do not think all the blame lies with Nathaniel,' she said carefully. 'I believe Lamorna had a mind of her own and she would not be led astray against her will.'

'He was the older of the two of them,' replied Seth. 'He should have known better.' He could not have known that to speak in such a way to a mother, a doting mother, about her offspring, was a dangerous thing to do. Eliza rose from the table. That Seth could speak in such a disapproving way of her beloved Nathaniel was a shock. That Seth, with whom she had usually such rapport, revealed himself to be totally out of sympathy with her was not something she could bear.

'I bid you goodnight,' she said in tones that could have frosted the windows in summer and swept out.

Next morning she decided it would be an opportune time to visit Austol. Both Seth and Barnabas had left for Wheal Rose and Rose herself was asleep after a bad night.

'I find it in my heart to be sorry for Lord Treloyhan,' commented Ewella as Eliza made ready to leave. 'One son a deserter from the army and a daughter in an untimely grave.'

Eliza did not acknowledge the remark. It seemed that Ewella and Morwenna Tregadillett had a similar penchant for gossip. What Kenwyn did was not their business. She herself had heard from Edgar that Kenwyn had been discharged because of ill health but he had not confided in his father. Austol of course jumped to the wrong conclusion and Kenwyn did not put him right. A streak of stubbornness ran through the whole family, Eliza reflected.

'I have taken the new hevvacake from the larder so please tell Mrs. Adwyn,' said Eliza. 'I am sure that Austol's girls are not eating properly – Edgar hinted as much.' Ewella nodded.

The journey to the Manor was uncomfortable in the extreme. A cold wind was blowing in from the sea and Eliza regretted that she had not asked for the carriage. Even Mathey, usually such a hardy soul, had resorted to a large moth-eaten scarf, his usual winter uniform, not one for spring, and Eliza wished she had thought to take a warmer shawl. Gratefully they turned into the long drive leading to the Manor. The rhododendrons, just coming into bloom in a profusion of red, white and deep lilac were a cheering sight and Eliza felt that she would be able to endure what promised to be a difficult visit.

She was shown into the morning room by a maid where Edgar rushed to greet her, a real smile of pleasure on his face

'Mistress Eliza, I am so glad to see you. At last we can try to cheer Austol and the girls. The maid will tell Mathey to go round to the kitchen and the cook will give him a warm drink. You both look frozen. It does not seem to be spring as yet.' The stream of chatter told Eliza that Edgar was nervous. 'Come to the chair by the fire and you will soon be warm. I shall go and tell Austol you are here – he and the girls have been gloomy for too long. The Tregadilletts did call but Austol refused to see them, saying that he was not yet ready to face the world. He has been spending a great deal of time up in the attics and I am not sure what he is doing. – but please wait in the morning room and I will fetch him.' Edgar bustled off, so unlike the suave self-assured persona he usually displayed that Eliza wondered what on earth was going on. He returned some minutes later looking very awkward.

'Mistress Eliza, would you be kind enough to attend Austol in the attic where Lamorna did her painting? I am so sorry but he was insistent.'

23

Faced with a closed door, Eliza took a deep breath and tapped on it. Then she entered, having heard nothing from the other side. A scene of unbelievable chaos met her eyes. Most of Lamorna's paintings had been taken down from the walls and left in a heap of mangled wood and canvas, some still complete, some ripped and spoiled, witness to Austol's temper and grief. Austol himself was standing by the window, turning when he heard Eliza. He fixed her with such a look of despair that it brought tears to her eyes.

'Why have you destroyed so many paintings?' she asked gently. 'I would have expected you to keep them?'

'I have kept only two,' replied Austol, his voice raw. 'I want nothing of her painting when she was with Nathaniel – that would be an unpleasing reminder. But I have kept one that is radically different,' and he gestured to the one that had made such an impression on Eliza previously.

'See the dark colours and the violent shapes? It is Lamorna's state of mind at the time she painted it, of that I am sure. It is a painting of quality and I intend to keep it in memory of her. But that is all. The rest – 'he gestured towards the pile of canvases 'is rubbish – inspired by a callow youth who did not recognise the value of the girl he led to her death.'

Eliza stepped back in horror. From being grief stricken, the underlying anger had emerged; he was consumed by anger. But she would not allow him to accuse Nathaniel only.

'Lamorna was a determined young lady and I am sure she would not easily be led!'

'Maybe. But he did not take care of her – he should have done!'

'She had run away from him to another 'friend' pointed out Eliza, but in milder tones. Austol was clearly nearly out of his mind, distraught with the happenings of the last few days. But there was more. His face became suffused with crimson and he spat out

'YOU are the one who does not understand! I am not being fair you tell me – but I have lost my only real daughter!'

'What do you mean? You have all those lovely girls still.'

'They are all the daughters of that pernicious creature, Eulalia! The bane of my life. I had to pretend I loved her but I only ever loved one woman – my beautiful Jenifer and Lamorna is HER daughter, hers and mine! I have done my utmost to treat her like the others – no favouritism, you understand. Unfortunately she has – had – an independent streak, just like her mother and we clashed too often.' He looked at Eliza's puzzled face and laughed harshly. 'A piece of Treloyhan family history you did not hear from my brother, obviously!'

'But I thought Jenifer died and then you married Eulalia?'

'She did not die, she ran away. She ran away from me. I loved her completely, I gave her everything she asked for – and still she ran away. Austol's voice had dropped to a whisper.' But she came back and it was as if we had never been apart. Of course there was Eulalia.' So much bitterness in that phrase. Poor Eulalia was Eliza's reaction. But Austol swept on, powered by grief. 'Because of Eulalia my lovely Jenifer had to give birth to our daughter on her own at the house of a friend. And THEN she died.' He stopped and stared out of the window. Eliza felt helpless in the face of such a cauldron of grief and anger and did not know what to say.

Then all at once, Austol wheeled round.

'Come with me. I have something for you to see.' He led Eliza into the attic that she knew was his own private gallery. Again there was devastation, portraits piled one on another in haphazard fashion in the middle of the floor, looking like a bonfire ready for burning. There was one portrait still hanging and Eliza caught her breath. She knew which one it was – the portrait of Jenifer.

'Do you see? My Jenifer – and here you are, so like her she might have returned from the grave!' Eliza shuddered. Austol was working himself up into a state of uncontrollable rage and she did not know what to do with him. She began to back towards the door.

'Let us go down to the drawing room and try some more of that brandy you have,' she said nervously. 'It will make you feel better.' Even to her own ears she sounded weak. Austol did not seem to hear her. He looked at her with eyes that did not really see her, a look reminiscent of Grace going through a bad patch. For Austol it was a look that rewrote his reality. A glitter of determination replaced the blankness and he made a sudden lunge, grabbing her by the arm. She found herself close – too close – to him, pressed against him so that she could smell the cigar smoke on his breath and the scented macassar oil he used on his hair. Roughly he tilted her head and his whiskers scratched her face. She knew he was going to kiss her – or maybe she was Jenifer in his mind – but the thought was unbearable. She managed to utter a feeble scream then he put a hand over her mouth.

'No one will hear you, my dear,' he hissed. 'We are three floors up and only Edgar is in this part of the house and he would not dare to disturb me!' He pushed her and she stumbled to the bare boards of the floor. He leaned over her, smiling a smile that was no smile. It was a signal of intent. Eliza realised that for the moment – praying it would be only a moment – he was insane! She made a move to scramble to her feet but he pinned her arms to the ground. Over six feet tall and strong he held her down with ease.

'Austol – what would Jenifer say if she knew what you were trying to do!' Eliza quavered. 'assaulting me will not bring back Lamorna you know that! What would she think of you! And I am Eliza, not Jenifer!' Austol knelt down beside her and spoke, every word like a hammer blow.

'Jenifer? I know YOU are Jenifer returned to me. When I met you at Roscarne I knew who you were. I tried to entice you back to the Manor but you were flirting with Seth. You should not have done that. First Barnabas – then Seth. Who else? You always were a loose woman at heart!' He wrapped her hair around his fingers, shedding pins and clips, and pulled. The pain brought tears to her eyes.

'Too late for tears now. You have to pay for what you did.'

'I have done nothing,' stammered Eliza. 'You are punishing the wrong person! Jenifer is no longer here. She is dead!' The word 'dead' seemed to bring Austol up short.

'NO!' he snapped. 'She is not dead! YOU are Jenifer.'

'I am Mistress Eliza Trevannion and my husband is Barnabas Trevannion of Roscarne,' Eliza said, as steadily as she could in such an undignified position. She tried hard to hide the fear that possessed her, despising her feelings of weakness and wishing she could assert herself. It was monstrous that Austol should treat her this way. Wriggle as she might, there was no chance of escape. Her heavy skirts hindered her and her boots were not solid enough to kick him, being of soft kid leather.

There came a knock at the door and Edgar's voice reached them.

'Austol? Mistress Eliza? Are you coming down for tea? It is ready and the girls seem to be hungry.' Eliza breathed a sigh of relief. Surely now she was safe. But she had reckoned without Austol, who was back in his world.

'We shall be down soon but I am telling Mistress Eliza the stories behind some of these pictures. Please do not disturb us.' His voice betrayed nothing. No menace, no disturbance, no anger. The footsteps went away. The smile Austol gave Eliza was of triumph.

'Now listen to me. What is going to happen to you is our secret. I shall not reveal to anyone that you and I – '

'I shall tell Barnabas!' choked Eliza.

'Then I shall withdraw all my investments in the consortium and persuade some of my friends to do the same. Your husband will not be pleased. He will be inclined to feel the fault is yours. You did come to see me here at the Manor after all.'

'But I'm NOT Jenifer,' Eliza trembled.

Austol's reply was to rip her cambric blouse, revealing her chemise, and to lever himself over her, blotting out the light in the room. Again Eliza tried to scream but to no avail. She felt her strength ebbing. Why was she so powerless? Then help came from an unexpected quarter. With a loud crash the portrait of Jenifer fell on to the bare floor.

24

The journey back to Roscarne was totally silent. Eliza sat straight-backed and uttered not a sound, which worried Mathey. When they arrived she hurried in to the house without a word of thanks, most unlike her.

'Somethin' up wi' Mistress Eliza, no doubt about that,' he confided to Trembles as he loosed the horse and put the trap away. 'Not somethin' nice neither. P'raps she might not go to the Manor so often. Never did like that Lord Treloyhan.'

Eliza, meanwhile, looking neither to right nor left, climbed the stairs to her special room, ignoring Nessa and Richard as she passed them. Nessa looked after her, big eyed with surprise and Richard had to comfort her by suggesting that Eliza was thinking about something. Which indeed she was. She felt soiled just remembering that dreadful scene with Austol and guilty at the same time. Perhaps she had been too ready to visit the Manor in answer to Austol's persistent demands and he had misunderstood her motivation. Those girls needed a mother not visits from a distant relation. And Austol? She shuddered. Yet there would be no possibility of avoiding him completely while he was threatening to remove his investment in the mines and break up the consortium. How could she bear it? The feel of his heavy body on hers was a nightmare that would not easily leave her, the smell of his cigar, the mad glint in his eye were all imprinted on her mind. Thank goodness for the timely interruption of Jenifer's portrait and the shock it gave Austol so that he loosened his grip on his victim and she was able to scramble away. Then there was Seth. Austol, so fixated on her, had picked up on her feelings for Seth. Perhaps she WAS a loose woman. Of course he was unhinged by his grief for Lamorna and was lashing out in all directions. This did not make Eliza feel any better. She could not pour out her woes to Barnabas. Apart from the fact that his first concern seemed to be Selena, which made her own place in his life so uncertain, he would scold her for going against his advice to let Austol solve his problems on his own. He would fly into one of his rages and her efforts to maintain ties with the Manor would come to nothing.

Eliza gradually became calmer as she gazed out to sea, a sea of improbable fairytale blue. She decided that she would put the episode behind her but she would take care never to visit Austol alone, even if it meant dragging an unwilling Uncle Tobias with her. She would concentrate on her own household and her own children and Austol and Edgar would have to manage as best they could. Nathaniel was still a pale ghost of himself and needed attention; Nessa was always so cheerful and obedient that Eliza realised that she did not really know what was going on in the little girl's mind. That would have to be remedied. Joel was possibly more biddable since his time as 'hero' but John and Caroline were both unusually quiet. She needed to find out how they were feeling about Nathaniel and Lamorna as so far little had been said. She decided to talk to Miss Maisie first but fate had other ideas. In the entrance hall she met Grace who had been for a walk, a short one as she complained about the cold even though she was wearing a fur lined hood. What she said agitated Eliza yet again.

'Rose said that Seth always seemed to be busy and somewhere else. I explained to Rose that that you and Seth seem to have become very close! He was probably talking to you!' The sweetness of her voice and the light way she spoke denied the spite in what she had confided.

'Grace! Why did you say such a thing to Rose? You know she is so easily upset these days!' Eliza exclaimed. Grace looked sulky. 'Well, it is true isn't it? There is nothing wrong in being good friends, is there? If that is all it is.'

'Of course that is all!' Eliza felt that the breath had been knocked out of her and her denial lacked conviction. 'Grace, how COULD you,' she whispered.

Grace shrugged. 'We were just talking,' she said and swept past her sister, her skirts rustling as she made her way up the stairs. A slight smile played about her lips.

'Eliza, where did you get those scratches?' It was Barnabas and beside him a smirking Selena.

'Oh, I fell in the shrubbery – no doubt I shall come out in bruises as well,' Eliza said, hurriedly. Selena looked at her, eyes narrowed to slits.

'You have just come back from the Manor?' she queried, innocently.' Was it in the Manor gardens you fell?'

'No!'

'Selena, it does not matter where,' interrupted Barnabas. 'I am concerned because Eliza looks shaken up. Sometimes a fall can be a shock to the body. You look quite white, my dear. I think you should lie down before supper.'

'Yes, I will do that,' said Eliza. There had been no distrustful overtones in her husband's voice, only consideration for her well-being. Grace had not spread her poison thus far, she thought, with relief. But supper that evening was an uneasy affair. Barnabas and Seth were there, Rose had come down from her room and even Grace put in an appearance. There was some mention of Nathaniel still feeling grief stricken and unable to eat but apart from that, talk was desultory. Eliza hardly dared look at Rose. However she was conscious of Seth glancing her way rather too often and she was relieved when the meal was over.

'Eliza, you have eaten very little,' said Ewella.

'She had a fall,' Barnabas put in. 'I am going to take her up to her room now and see that she is comfortable.'

'But – ' began Selena.

'Later, Mistress Selena.' said Barnabas coldly. He did not like his decisions to be questioned. He put his arm around Eliza and led her from the room, followed by Uncle Tobias.

'Perhaps some of my special brandy would help,' suggested the old man kindly.'
'Excellent idea. We shall come to your study and I shall take Eliza up afterwards.'
There followed a congenial little gathering of three, warmed by best French brandy. If only Barnabas was always like this, Eliza thought, as she drifted into a healing sleep.

The next morning she was late down to breakfast and disturbed to find Seth waiting for her.
'Are you well?' he asked anxiously. 'You did look strained last night.'
'I am better,' Eliza said in cool tones. She had not forgiven him for his remarks about Nathaniel. Seth moved to take her hands in his but then thought better of it.
'I want to apologise for my outburst the other day,' he said awkwardly. 'It was thoughtless of me and the only excuse I have is tiredness after a bad day at Wheal Rose.'
Eliza nodded. Desperately she wanted to confide in Seth about Austol and his behaviour but she knew how much he disapproved of her visits to the Manor. He would be less than sympathetic. Who could she turn to? And could she tell him what Grace had intimated to Rose? These thoughts swirled round her mind as she hurried down the path to the shore. Being next to the sea was always a remedy for a troubled mind and she determined to walk as far as Marah Cove, aiming to banish the memory of poor Lamorna lying there with a distraught Nathaniel bending over her. She wanted to reclaim the beauty of the cove as a place where she could find peace of mind and comfort as before. She was brought up short as she reached Marietta Cove. It seemed to her that the pile of stones and rubble at the foot of the cliffs had increased. Another cliff fall had certainly occurred. On her return she would report it to Barnabas.

Finally she reached Marah Cove. She perched on a rock and watched the waves chase each other to the shore in a never ending restless advance and retreat and gradually she began to feel calmer. It was not to last.

'Eliza. I hoped you would be here.' It was Edgar, smart in his revenue man's uniform. He looked relaxed and positively handsome Eliza was pleased to see. Here was one who had recovered from a difficult time.

'Ewella said that you had come down to the sea for a walk. I was worried about you after your last visit to the Manor. Austol has been in such a dreadful mood that I was sure something had happened?' Eliza scrutinised him suspiciously. No, Edgar's face was open and enquiring. He did not know what Austol had done – or tried to do. He was the perfect confidant, someone who did not want something from her and would not reveal her secrets.

'Edgar, may I talk to you in confidence?'

'Of course.' He sat down on another rock and prepared to listen. As Eliza proceeded, he looked more and more horrified.

'We all understand how Austol must be grieving for Lamorna,' he said, slowly. 'But I think there is even more than that affecting the state of his mind. He has not forgotten Jenifer, Lamorna's mother – '

'No, and he seems to have some wild idea that I look like her,' said Eliza crossly. 'I was beginning to think that he had designs on me for that very reason. I have never felt comfortable in his presence and now I know why. Heaven knows what unlikely ideas he has been dragging out of the depths of his mind!'

25

'There is something you should know,' said Edgar, as they walked slowly back across the sand. 'Austol has thrown out all of Lamorna's paintings – they are in a pile outside waiting for the grounds-man to light a bonfire.'

'Surely he will regret that when his grief has subsided?'

'That's not all. He is disposing of all his own collection and says that he does not wish to collect portraits as of now and will not open a gallery as he had intended'

'What about that portrait of Jenifer?' Eliza could hardly believe what she had just heard. Edgar shrugged. 'I don't know about that but I feel that burning Lamorna's paintings is wrong. I hate to think how Nathaniel will feel when he finds out.' Eliza nodded.

'We should stop him,' she said. 'Edgar, I need you to do something for me as I cannot possibly communicate with Austol at the moment. Could you persuade Jean Luc to come over and save the best paintings – then Nathaniel and I could offer to pay for them?'

Edgar looked doubtful. 'We could try. I shall go to see Jean Luc as soon as I can. And I shall have a word with the grounds-man!'

Jean Luc was only too willing to pay a visit to the Manor.

'To destroy zose paintings – sacrilege! They 'ave talent and I could put them – some of them' – he amended hastily 'in my 'ouse. Summer is coming and tourists also. I pay commission to Lord Treloyhan or le pauvre Nathaniel!' Edgar did his best to explain the difficult circumstances at the Manor but Jean Luc waved them away.

'No matter! I will bring my best brandy as a gift. It will soften ze hardest heart! You see, Lord Treloyhan and Jean Luc will become the best of friends!'

He was as good as his word. He arrived early one afternoon, whiskers waxed, wearing a beret and a multi-coloured cloak and with a bottle under each arm, demanding to see Lord Treloyhan. Possibly overcome by his bizarre appearance and unusual accent, the parlour maid showed him into the morning room. At first Austol refused to see him but Jean Luc wore down the maid with Gallic charm and she did her best. An irritable Austol was no match for a determined Jean Luc who obtained permission to salvage some of Lamorna's paintings; moreover Austol was left in a resigned and slightly more mellow mood.

Back at Roscarne, a shaken Eliza knew that she had several problems to deal with, counting them off on her fingers. She and Barnabas needed to be closer. Selena was the stumbling block and somehow the girl had to be detached from her husband. Certainly Nathaniel had to be coaxed out of his crippling grief but all the children were in need of attention; she had hardly spoken to John since his return from school, then poor red eyed anxious Caroline, smiley Nessa and mischievous Joel all needed their mother. So did Richard but he had given up trying to reach his own mother and always confided in Eliza. But what of Grace? Her sister had an uncanny ability to spark trouble and now she had detected the connection between Seth and Eliza there was no limit to what she might say. Eliza drew in a deep breath. Seth. The name alone had been synonymous with warmth and pleasure and, it had to be admitted, love. Yet his presence at Roscarne had not brought them closer, rather the reverse. She looked at the sea which whispered outside her window, a sea which suffered storms and calms like humans did, yet there was no comfort there for her, an erring human. And Rose? Her good friend Rose who did not know that her husband loved another woman. Eliza heaved a deep sigh. Her conscience told her that she should honour her friendship with Rose as well as her marriage vows to Barnabas and put an end to this increasingly risky relationship. She knew that Seth was torn two ways also – the attention needed by his sickly wife and his friendship with Barnabas. In a moment of clarity Eliza realised that she was damaging the fabric of Roscarne as surely as if she were tearing threads from a valuable tapestry.

There was no sign of Nathaniel or Caroline in the house which was frustrating as Eliza wanted to embark on her crusade straight away. But Barnabas and Seth were at Wheal Rose and the children were in the schoolroom with Miss Maisie. And Selena? No, she did not want to see Selena. Nor did she want to think about Austol and the Manor, no not for a long while. She decided that she would walk to Marah Cove instead and try to erase the memory of a grieving Nathaniel kneeling beside the body of Lamorna. So sad to lose her in such a way. So young to have his heart broken.

There was no sign of Nathaniel as she rounded the cliff fall, but perched on the rock where she herself had sat so often was Caroline.

'I have been following Nathaniel, Mama,' she explained. 'He is in such a low state that I do not think he is responsible for what he is doing.'

'What IS he doing?'' Alarm sounded in her voice.

'He is painting this cove from all angles and at all states of the tide. He says it will help him to remember her and when I said what about the portrait you have of her he made a face and insisted what he was doing was the best way!'

'Where is he now?'

'As the tide is right out he is on the extreme end of this tumble of rocks – look, you can just see him from here. I warned him about the tide and how it can surround him so silently but he said he was quite aware of that. Oh Mama, I am so frightened for him! He gets lost in his painting and will forget to keep watch. The sea is a beast licking its lips and waiting for him!'

'Caroline, you underestimate your brother. He has lived in Roscarne for most of his life! He knows about tides and rough seas. If doing these paintings is helping him to assuage his grief, we should let him.' Eliza reached out and patted her daughter on the shoulder. But Caroline was not to be comforted. She turned to look at her mother, her eyes brilliant with unshed tears.

'This place – so beautiful to see but underneath it is menacing. I feel there is cruelty here and a coldness I don't feel elsewhere. Maybe Lamorna is looking for Nathaniel.' Her voice broke. An alarmed Eliza spoke firmly:

'Caroline, keep that imagination of yours under control,' she said. 'I know you can sense more than most of us but after this dreadful tragedy it is not surprising that you worry. Leave Nathaniel to his painting and walk with me to Ros Sands. Look, the tide is not yet on the turn, it is still going out.'

They walked slowly on towards the pretty bay known as Ros Sands but Eliza could see that Caroline was still jumpy. The sun was in benign mood and the breeze gentle but the shadow of poor Lamorna had cast a blight that even the kind spring weather could not dissipate. The walk did nothing to calm Caroline but on their return they could see Nathaniel trudging ahead of them and at last she could smile. 'I will go and catch him up!' she exclaimed and darted off.

Eliza walked slowly, following her first born twins and hoping that Caroline would be instrumental in helping to heal Nathaniel. A visit to Uncle Tobias would be an antidote to all this worry she decided. He seemed delighted to see her, but his first words presented a challenge.

'Eliza, my dear, when are you visiting the Manor again? A message has arrived from Austol who wishes to see you.'

'Oh no, Uncle, I have been too often to the Manor recently,' stammered Eliza. The old man looked surprised. 'I was hoping to accompany you – I should like to convey my sympathy to him in person. It was unfortunate that I was not well enough to attend the funeral.'

'Who brought the message, Uncle?' quavered Eliza.

'Kenwyn. He has turned out to be such a nice boy. I do not believe all that tosh about him being a deserter. I tackled him about that and he admitted it was not so but his father was so ready to believe the worst of him he decided to let him. A punishment!'

'Fathers and sons seem to have difficult relationships at times,' agreed Eliza. 'I hope you told him to put it right!'

'That I did – but I wonder if he will do so. I am sorry you do not wish to visit the Manor just now but do tell me when you decide to go.' He fell into a disappointed silence. It was not often Uncle Tobias made any request at all so Eliza knew she could not refuse him.

What came next was a bolt from the blue. She was taking tea with Rose who was in thoughtful mood.

'Eliza I need to tell you what I – we – are planning!' She began. 'I am so much better and it is only these stupid megrims that are bothering me now. Seth and I both feel that we should move into a house of our own and stop being a burden on you all at Roscarne.'

26

'Of course you are not a burden!' Eliza managed. 'I do realise that you would like to be independent – ' But she did not understand. Had Seth made the suggestion? The thought made her heart sink.

'We would not move too far away,' Rose said eagerly 'I feel I should enjoy finding a place of our own and I am sure Seth would agree with me. I must be so much better or I would not even contemplate such a move!'

Eliza was in the kitchen helping Mrs. Adwyn by peeling potatoes. The mindless occupation allowed her to muse on what had just happened. She could not believe that Seth would suggest leaving Roscarne without prompting from Rose. Did Rose then take notice of Grace's spiteful words? It would be like her friend not to bring it out into the open but quietly remove her husband from temptation. It would be the right decision but could she, Eliza, bear it? Could Seth face leaving Roscarne? Such ideas as she herself had toyed with were acceptable in the abstract. But to find them actually happening? Mrs. Adwyn opened her mouth to thank Eliza for her help but kept silent, deterred by the look on Eliza's face. Something was very wrong.

'Seth and Rose want to leave us!' Barnabas announced to Eliza as they made ready for bed. 'I understand their reasons but we shall miss them.'

'It is good to know that Rose feels strong enough to face setting up house somewhere else,' murmured Eliza. 'I thought her megrims were still worrying her but apparently not.'

'She has you to thank for looking after her,' Barnabas said approvingly, unaware that he was heaping coals of fire on his wife's head. 'Somehow I feel that Grace, however, will never be well enough to move and she will always remain here, a prospect that I view with some trepidation!'

'We do have plenty of space,' Eliza replied acidly.

They met in the morning room after breakfast. Eliza turned to make a hasty escape but Seth held on to her arm. 'Please sit down for a minute,' he said gently. 'I need you to know that I did not make the suggestion to leave. It was Rose's idea. Of course I am pleased that she feels so much better but I am overwhelmed with sadness at the prospect of parting from Roscarne – and yet it is for the best.'

'How so?' faltered Eliza.

'Where are we going? We both have others who are dependent on us, good people, whom we cannot let down. And you have children also! You could not leave them neither could you take them away from Barnabas. We have known this from the beginning but have been ready to swim along with the tide as long as we could see each other and look forward to the occasional contact. I may say this has been a refined form of torture for me.'

'And me,' sighed Eliza. 'At the same time I would throw myself on the floor and scream for you to stay if it would do any good. But you have made up your mind have you not?'

Seth nodded. 'I feel we should do this before someone is irretrievably hurt or our love for each other is sullied by thoughtless talk. But we shall still see each other. I shall encourage Rose to seek a house not too far away.' Eliza gazed at him in despair.

'We shall see very little of each other!' she burst out. 'Austol and Grace already realise we are too close! They and Morwenna Tregadillett are like pigs rooting for morsels of gossip!'

Seth laughed. 'I shall always envisage them as the three pigs now. Eliza, you have a picturesque turn of phrase!' Unwillingly she smiled.

Rose managed to propound an even worse idea when she and Eliza were chatting in the drawing room. It was true that suddenly Rose looked much better. There was pink in her cheeks and she looked trim and attractive in a new green dress, a colour which had always suited her. The prospect of house hunting had energised her.

'If Wheal Rose runs into difficulties – and so many of the mines around here are closing – I shall suggest that we return to Arizona. It will not be so bad if we have a proper house and are not forced to live in a shack like last time!' she laughed merrily, a laugh that did not ring true. Eliza tried hard to keep a sympathetic smile on her face as her spirits plummeted. Arizona! Then she would never see Seth again!

'What about Barnabas and the consortium?' she asked cautiously. 'I know my husband relies on Seth a great deal – ' Rose frowned and looked uncomfortable.

'I had not thought of that,' she said. 'But of course we each have to look after our own families, do we not? Barnabas would not grudge us making the best of our chances?'
Eliza gazed at her friend thoughtfully. This was not the same Rose she had always known. At one time she would have considered the welfare of everyone around her, not just her own needs. But then she herself was so different from the early days.

They were interrupted by the arrival of Caroline, her dark hair in disarray and again tears in her eyes.

'Mama,' she cried. 'Please could I have a word with you?' Discreetly Rose left and Caroline plumped herself down next to her mother. It turned out that the tears in her eyes were from temper not grief, unusual for Caroline.

'That Selena!' she said. 'All I did was ask her how long she intended staying at Roscarne and what she was intending to do – and she turned on me, spitting like a cat. She said she had no intention of leaving in the near future and would probably still be here when I left! She said that if Mr. Barnabas was pleased to welcome her to Roscarne that was all that mattered. She said that she did not care what anyone else thought! The cheek of it!'

'Perhaps it was a little tactless to ask when she was leaving?' suggested her mother. 'I do know how you feel, Caroline. I am resentful that she is still here after all this time – but if her presence is what Barnabas desires, what can we do?'

'I shall tackle Papa myself. Perhaps he will give me his reasons.'

'Be careful of that temper of his!' said Eliza. 'Now, changing the subject, how is Nathaniel faring? Do you think he is beginning to get over losing Lamorna?'
Caroline made a face. 'Not really. I found out that he still goes every day to paint from the rocks in Marah Cove. I thought he had finished with all that. But he seems obsessed still.'

'Perhaps we should take a walk to Marah Cove and see what he is doing,' said Eliza. 'Perhaps we could divert him – he could paint you instead, Caroline!' Her daughter managed a smile.

'I do not like going to Marah Cove, Mama,' she protested. 'It gives me the chills even when the sun is shining.'

'I know what you mean. But if we can help Nathaniel it will be a worthwhile outing.' As it happened the sun was not shining. It was a pale grey day, the sky covered in light cloud and the sea unruffled by the wind. The yellow of the scar on the cliff was muted and even the gulls seemed to be less clamorous, drifting idly by, only their white feathers still bright against sea and sky.

'The tide is right out – much further than usual,' said Caroline.

'Spring tides do that,' said Eliza abstractedly. Though worried about Nathaniel she could not get Seth out of her mind nor banish Rose's new defiant gaze and implacable intentions. Seth would do as she wanted, so guilt ridden was he about his marriage to her.

'There he is!' cried Caroline as Nathaniel appeared, negotiating the rocks with ease even though he was carrying his fold away easel and his portfolio of paintings under his arm. Eliza was heartened to see him smile briefly at his mother and sister and then jump down on to the sand.

'Look Mama, Caroline!' he said eagerly.' Look at this painting!' They looked and Caroline could not resist a cry of concern. Eliza was horrified. The painting showed sea and sky and rocks, and the tide flooding in bearing with it a figure with white face and trailing hair. He had painted Lamorna.

27

'Do not look so horrified, Mama,' scolded Nathaniel. 'This is the best painting I have ever done! See the light on the water, the threatening colour of the sky, the elegant curve of the body! Millais painted Ophelia lying in water but he had his model posing in a bath!'

'But your – er – body is not posing. It is real!' Eliza protested gently.

'Are you comparing yourself to the famous painter John Everett Millais?' Caroline broke in, incredulous. Her brother seemed to have lost all humility. Furthermore he seemed to have distanced himself from the tragedy that led to his painting.

'You don't understand! I was inspired! Lamorna inspired me!' Nathaniel's face flushed red as a febrile excitement gripped him. Eliza did not know what to say. Her son seemed so far away from her and she suffered a momentary flash of rage that Barnabas had insisted on sending him to school away from home. She knew that his exile contributed to this isolation from her and the rest of the family. She looked again at the painting. It drew her, pulled her towards the reality behind it. Any minute she felt the body would turn its head and Lamorna would smile at them, tossing her heavy, water sodden hair over her shoulder. Her eyes would turn glassy green and her languorous mouth open to reveal pearly teeth as white as the wavelets that broke over her. Eliza felt the colour leave her face at the thought.

'We should all return to the house and let the others see your painting.' said Caroline.' Mama looks so tired now. She should not be out any longer.' Nathaniel nodded. 'Yes of course, but I shall not come with you. I shall take the pony

and trap to Newlyn and go to see Jean Luc. He will tell me if I have done well and I trust his judgement.'
'Then I shall come with you?' Tired or not, Eliza did not want to let him out of her sight.
'You may both come though it will be rather crowded in the trap!'

Jean Luc opened his door to them with a smile of surprise. After polite introductions Nathaniel could contain himself no longer.
'I have a painting for you – I need your opinion!' Gravely Jean Luc unrolled the thick paper and gave an exclamation when he saw the subject. Then he said nothing as he scrutinized Nathaniel's handiwork. Eliza and Caroline watched him, Caroline with a dubious expression on her face. Finally, with exaggerated care, he handed the picture back to Nathaniel. Still he said nothing. Then he ushered the three of them to his studio where so many famous names decorated the walls. He bade them sit down at the rickety wooden table where he entertained his guests and, with a flourish, opened a bottle of cognac.
'Now we celebrate!'
'Celebrate?' Nathaniel's voice shook just a little.
'Mais oui! To celebrate the discovery of one who will be a great painter. One who is able to use what 'appens in his life, 'owever tragic, to produce great art! Nathaniel, your painting has given me grand plaisir and I believe it ees the beginning of a career that will make your family proud of you. 'Also,' he paused for a moment. 'We celebrate the life of your friend, the sad Lamorna. All life, however short should be a cause for celebration. She would have been so pleased that you honoured her in death as you loved her in life! Zis way you will never forget her – never!'
Eliza and Caroline were rendered speechless by this outpouring of praise for Nathaniel who had received nothing but criticism from Austol and Barnabas. The boy's spine unfurled like a plant receiving water and he stood straight,

losing the stoop of grief and uncertainty. Solemnly they stood and drank to Lamorna and then they turned to Nathaniel and toasted him. The cognac warmed and cheered them before they took their leave; the painting Nathaniel left with Jean Luc who intended to take it to London, to the Royal Academy no less.

'I shall enter it for the Summer Exhibition where it will be noticed for sure. He paints in the style of Waterhouse who is exhibiting at the Royal Academy right now!' In his excitement the exaggerated French slant to his conversation so carefully maintained to impress his buyers, escaped Jean Luc. He patted Nathaniel on the shoulder and pretended not to notice the tears which sprang to the boy's eyes.

'Please do not speak of this visit to anyone at all, Mama – nor you Caroline. I wish to wait and see what the academicians have to say. They may not feel the same way as Jean Luc.'

'I am so pleased for you!' squealed Caroline, taking her place again as the first lady in his life. She knew perfectly well that another Lamorna would come along in the future and she would be relegated to second place but for the time being she would always be by Nathaniel's side. Eliza, however, was musing over other problems as they rattled towards Roscarne. How would Austol react to a painting of his drowned daughter? And how would Barnabas receive the account of recent events? There was deep water ahead.

'Ewella, I have to visit the Manor again. An important matter.' Eliza tried and failed to sound brisk and determined. She knew what Ewella would say. And she did.

'Surely Mistress Eliza it would be most inappropriate for you to do so. Barnabas is away somewhere with that Selena – '

'Just as well,' interrupted Eliza. 'You and I both know he would not let me go. But please believe me, Ewella, it is a necessary visit. If he returns before I do, please say that you do not know where I am.' She looked appealingly at her sister-in-law

'Yes, well, if you insist,' said Ewella grudgingly.

'Ewella I do not know what I should do without you.' Eliza hurried out to warn Mathey that she needed the pony and trap, leaving Ewella surprised and smiling at such an accolade.

A maid showed her into the drawing room where Austol was sitting staring into space, not even pretending to read the book on his lap.

'Well, Mistress Eliza, I did not expect to see you again so soon,' was his gruff greeting. But there was no hiding that he was a man much diminished, a shark with no teeth.

'I did not to expect to come here ever again!' said Eliza coldly. 'But I have something important to tell you, during which time I expect you to behave like a gentleman. I should remind you that I have left word at Roscarne that I am visiting you and they will come for me if I am too long.' She had a brief vision of Ewella coming to her aid and had to restrain a grin. Austol regarded her, puzzled at her demeanour.

'What is this so important news?'

'It concerns Nathaniel and Lamorna'

'There is nothing more to be said,' Austol growled. 'I have lost my daughter and that is all.'

'Not quite. Nathaniel has painted her as he found her.' She held up her hand, to silence his outraged protest. 'It is a beautiful painting, if sad, and there is a likelihood of it being hung at the Summer Exhibition at the Royal Academy. Jean Luc was full of praises and intends to take it up to London. I felt that this should not happen behind your back and that is why I am here to tell you.' Not waiting for a response she rose to leave. Wearily, Austol stood also, his stance that of an old man.

'Jean Luc? A man who knows what he is talking about,' he muttered. Then, with a palpable effort he looked

straight at Eliza. 'I treated you so badly!' he said. 'And yet –
here you are. I am not sure how I feel about the painting but I
do know that I wish for your goodwill towards me. I was in
turmoil about so many things when last we met – though I
know that does not excuse the way I behaved.' Eliza nodded
curtly. She did not want to spend another second at the Manor
nor listen to his excuses. Her memories were still too raw.

Before she could leave, Kenwyn came in.

'Mistress Eliza it is good to see you. Tell me, how is
Caroline?'

'She is well, Kenwyn,' Eliza smiled. 'Though she is
finding Nathaniel's grief so upsetting.'

'Maybe I could help by diverting her attention
sometimes?' Kenwyn said eagerly. Eliza looked at him in
surprise, then came to a swift decision. 'Come to tea
tomorrow, Kenwyn. I am sure your father will agree?'

'Most kind of you Mistress Eliza,' said Austol with a
dour face.

28

Back at Roscarne the first person she met was Seth, looking serious.

'Come to the morning room, I should like to talk to you.'

'I am sorry, Seth, not now. We'll talk later. I need to find Caroline as I have invited Kenwyn to tea and she does not know.' She was almost babbling but she felt the need to ward off what he was going to say, feeling sure that it was something unpleasant.

'Kenwyn? Why on earth are you inviting Kenwyn? Is this another way to keep in touch with Austol?' Seth was angry.

'No, Seth. My idea is to stop Caroline following Nathaniel everywhere. Kenwyn is an attractive boy and he seems interested in her so I thought I would encourage him.'

'Eliza, you are playing with fire if you are matchmaking!' exclaimed Seth. 'But it is just like you. You want to fix everything with no thought for the consequences!'

'I am NOT matchmaking!' retorted Eliza. 'Caroline is only fifteen – '

'Nearly sixteen!' interrupted Seth. 'And Kenwyn is twenty one I believe – and a deserter from his regiment!'

'Apparently he is NOT a deserter. I do not understand why he should continue with this falsehood. I intend to ask him.'

Seth sighed in exasperation, but before he could say anything else, Eliza hurried off, leaving him unsure whether he was angry with her or admiring of the way she tried to look after her family.

At last he managed to trap her in the morning room.

'Eliza!' he took her hands in his. 'We have talked about Rose and I moving away from here.'

'Yes.'

'There is something else. Rose declares that she would like to return to Arizona.'

'And you? '

He shrugged. 'Wheal Rose is working successfully and I feel I am not needed in the same way.' Through the roaring in her ears Eliza managed to stutter 'But I need you!'

'That, my dear, is why we must go.'

Alone in the morning room, Eliza could not assimilate what had just happened to her. For Seth and Rose to move out at all was bad enough but to go to the other side of the world where she and Seth would never see each other was a blow hard to bear. And it was the second time he would be leaving her. How could he do that? She had fought her way through grief once before and it was beyond belief that it should happen again. She curled up in an armchair and covered her face with her hands. It was this way that Grace found her.

'Eliza, what is wrong?' she sounded genuinely concerned.

'Just not feeling well.' Eliza struggled up. 'I shall go to lie down for a while. Will you tell Ewella I shall not be down for supper?' Not waiting for an answer she made her escape.

'Mama?' It was Caroline. She always knew where to find her mother. 'John has been teasing Nessa and she is so upset! Could you come and see her? She will not listen to me.'

Eliza dragged herself out of the morass of despondency that was threatening to engulf her. She knew John could pinpoint weakness with unerring efficiency and it seemed he had done so with Nessa. Eliza found her in the room she shared with

Elestren, her face red with distress and large tears rolling down her face.

'Nessa! Whatever is the matter?'

'J – John said – I was too roly-poly for my new dress!' Nessa finally admitted. Eliza hid a smile.

'Go and put it on and I shall have a look at it,' she said gently. The seamstress from Rosmorren had been busy sewing new dresses for all the girls ready for the spring but Eliza had not yet seen Nessa's. Another maternal task that she had neglected. Reluctantly her daughter brought out a pretty dress of white muslin with a high lace collar and frilled sleeves and wriggled into it with a certain amount of difficulty. There was no doubt that the fit was too tight around the waist and it made her look plumper than she really was.

'Let me see – if we loosen this seam here and omit the gathers round the back it will be fine. I shall see to it myself and you will look lovely, I promise you!' Nessa smiled through her tears. If only her own problems could be so easily rectified, Eliza reflected.

For supper that evening, Eliza determined to put on a good face. Her real feelings she wanted to hide from Seth and Rose and indeed everyone. Barnabas would notice if she seemed quieter than usual and ask awkward questions while Ewella's sharp eyes missed nothing. Taking care with her appearance would armour her against speculation. She would wear her claret silk which made her eyes look violet and her only ornament would be a silver comb in her hair. She preened in front of the mirror, pleased by the way she looked. Having lost weight in the previous few difficult weeks her waist was minute and the gown swirled in elegant folds to the floor. True, her face was too pale and she had to pinch her cheeks for some colour but then she felt that she was ready to face everyone – even Seth. How false he would deem her if he knew her motivation, how shallow she was being. Perhaps she should rush back to her room and change into her grey twill dress? Too late. To her horror she found there were extra guests at the supper table. Barnabas had invited Austol and Edgar as there had been a meeting of the consortium that afternoon, an event Eliza had been too distraught to remember. Surely it was rather soon for Austol to mix socially but he seemed at ease though grief had marked his face with heavy lines. Barnabas had decided that Nathaniel and Caroline should take their supper with the younger children out of consideration for Austol's feelings and Eliza was grateful for his unusual sensitivity. She determined to talk to him after supper. Nessa had made her realise that she and Barnabas both had been neglecting the younger children in their concerns for Nathaniel. She had been guilty of spending too much time at the Manor and Barnabas? He was always out somewhere with Selena. Things would have to change she vowed grimly.

It was noticeable that Seth and Rose came down to supper in very different moods. Rose was alight with excitement but Seth was quiet and sombre, his face etched with downward lines and his dark eyes without their usual spark. He chatted quietly to Barnabas for a while then turned to Ewella who turned pink with pleasure. Eliza tried to talk to Selena, with little success so she turned her attention to Edgar. Fortunately Austol was in deep discussion with Uncle Tobias about some aspect of mining and the rumours of further closures in the district, releasing Eliza from the necessity of conversing with him. She was grateful when the meal drew to a close and she could make her escape. She would have liked to talk to Rose but her one time friend was evasive, talking animatedly to Austol and Eliza realised that Grace had well and truly dripped poison in her ear. Not poison of course. What she had insinuated was true. As she left, head held high, Seth darted one glance full of pain after her, a glance intercepted by Rose whose lips thinned.

There was only one place she could go. Her attic room beckoned as a haven of peace where her misdemeanours seemed less important in the wider world of sea and sky. She curled up in her armchair trying to lose herself in the beauty of the evening but thoughts would keep floating through her mind, thoughts which turned everything grey. She was to lose Seth and she had already lost her good friend Rose. But this paled beside her other weaknesses, neglecting her children, her infrequent visits to Uncle Tobias, her lack of care for Grace oh, her faults were legion. There was a tap at the door. It was Richard.

'I – I thought I might find you here,' he said. 'Please tell me if I am disturbing you.' He stood there, angelic with his blond hair and his mother's grey eyes, looking at her with a worried expression. She smiled with real warmth. Richard always made her smile. A ten year old with such caring and perception was unusual.

'I wanted to tell you how pretty you look!' he said in a rush. 'But you look so serious sometimes that I think something is wrong.'

'Nothing is wrong, Richard,' said Eliza, soothingly. 'Only the usual worries that everyone has. I want to see all the children before bedtime. Will you come with me?'

Again her good intentions came to nothing. She met Rose on the stairs who said without preamble 'I need to talk to you, Eliza. Can we go back up to the attic room as we are less likely to be disturbed?' Eliza's heart missed a beat. Richard looked at her in alarm then melted away, conscious that his beloved aunt had other concerns.

'Eliza, I know what I am doing to you,' said Rose, baldly. 'I did not want to say anything at first but just leave for Arizona. But we have had such a long friendship and you have shown me so many kindnesses that I cannot part from you just like that.' Eliza could say nothing. Her throat was dry and she wondered what was coming next.

'I know that you and Seth are – are attracted to each other.'

'Yes.'

'I understand it. Seth is a wonderful man and you – you were – you are my best friend.'

'Yes,' said Eliza, humbly. Then Rose said something surprising.

'He married me. But I knew at the time that he loved you. So I played you false back then. But I was envious of you with your children and your marriage to Barnabas and I thought that if Seth and I went away he would forget you. But he did not.'

'I am so sorry – '

'Neither of you can deny your feelings so the only thing to do is to live far apart and that is why I persuaded him to think of Arizona again.' Rose leaned forward and took Eliza's cold hands in hers. 'At first I hated you – but now I realise that our friendship is important. Neither of us intended to harm the other and we have years of happy times to look back on. Our separation will, hopefully, help us to settle down, you with Barnabas and me with Seth. But I hope you will always be my friend.'

29

The following week passed quickly. Rose was packing while Seth and Barnabas spent the time in conference about Wheal Rose and Wheal Eliza, sorting out investments and dividends, Barnabas becoming more and more gloomy. Seth was a friend, not just a business partner, and Barnabas did not really understand why he wanted to move to the other side of the world.

'It is for Rose,' Seth insisted. 'The sunshine in Arizona did her good before and will again. It was only because she was so homesick that we came back the first time. Gold mining is a growing occupation in Arizona while tin mining here in Cornwall is not. I fear that the whole industry will soon be suffering more competition from Australia and South Africa and it will not survive.'

'We have had problems before and succeeded in overcoming them,' Barnabas pointed out. 'Prices have been rising recently – '

'I am so sorry,' said Seth, sincerely. 'I do not want to leave you and the family, believe me. I shall miss the life in Cornwall. However Rose is my wife and I must do the best I can for her.'

Barnabas sighed. 'Of course. I would do the same for Eliza, but fortunately she thrives in Cornwall.'

The mention of Eliza bid fair to undermine Seth's defences and he changed the subject quickly.

Uncle Tobias was not pleased. He poured out his feelings to Eliza when she came to sit with him one evening. 'Seth and Barnabas are such good friends and they work well together. Surely Rose can see that! And she is your friend also! She should not go scuttling off to Arizona however warm the sunshine. It seems to me a very selfish action.' Eliza murmured agreement though she wondered what Uncle Tobias would say if he knew the real reason for the departure of the Quinns. The feeling of guilt shrouded her like a sea mist and though she kept herself busy with the children, Caroline for one realised that her mother was unhappy. She confided in Nathaniel who said that he thought it was all because of the death of Lamorna and the way that had affected so many people. Like many others, he arrogated blame to himself, not able to separate from his own personal concerns. Caroline was not so sure. Something else was upsetting her mother. Of course Rose had been a good friend for many years and the prospect of her leaving was sad – but then she would have voiced that sadness. Instead she was by turns overly cheerful and then quiet, her emotions tightly reined in.

It was time to say goodbye. Seth and Rose were taking the carriage to Penzance and from there they would catch the train to London. Then they would travel to Southampton and board one of the large liners leaving for New York. Large swathes of land and sea would separate them from Cornwall
And at the thought, Eliza felt her heart would break. Never to see either of them again? Never to laugh and share confidences with Rose? Never to see the affection in Seth's dark eyes and feel safe because he was there? How could she bear it? Rose took refuge in tears as she had done before while Seth shook hands with everyone crowded at the front door. He kissed Grace, who looked bewildered, then Ewella who blushed, then Eliza who closed her eyes. 'Courage' he whispered. 'It will not be for ever. We shall both return one day, I promise you!'

'Yes,' thought Eliza 'When we are all stooped and grey and old. What good is that when all these precious days will have passed, all wasted because we are not together?' All too soon the children had chorused their goodbyes and the carriage had rolled off down the drive, the uncaring sun shining brightly.

The household was very subdued after their departure. Uncle Tobias was visibly upset, Grace retired to sulk in her room and refused to come down for meals, Ewella and Mrs. Adwyn sat at the kitchen table with numerous cups of tea citing Seth's virtues in lugubrious tones and even the children were less boisterous. Barnabas could not believe that his friend, Seth, had actually gone and Eliza – well, Eliza moved round the house in a daze or sat up in her attic room and endured flashes of memory from former years – her long friendship with Rose when they were young, her first meeting with Seth down by the sea, their growing attraction for each other, the feeling of loss when he married Rose – so many memories.

What she did realize was that the distance between herself and Barnabas was not all his fault. He had received less than her total attention, much less, so the advent of Selena was inevitable and she knew that the first thing she had to do was reinstate herself as the first lady in his life and dispatch Selena. How, she did not know. It was difficult to think with such a headache. It was difficult to look out of the window at the sea this particular morning because sunlight on the water was dazzling; her skin radiated heat and she had vague pains in her arms and legs and no desire to move from her chair. She closed her eyes. It was Caroline who found her and hurried down to Ewella.

'Mama, I think she is ill,' she said breathlessly. 'She won't talk to me and she looks very poorly.'

'Influenza,' said Dr. Trevell when he finally arrived. 'Put her to bed, supply plenty of fluids and do not let the younger children near her. There have been several cases in the village and three of the girls at the Manor have caught it.'

It was Barnabas who carried Eliza down to their bedroom and put her to bed, frightened by her pallor and her inability to speak. She just moaned and swallowed the water Ewella supplied, then lay still with her eyes closed. Barnabas moved a chair beside the bed so that he could monitor his wife and prepared to wait. It seemed to him that Roscarne was enduring one blow after another and this last was worst of all for him. Eliza was never ill. She was always there at the centre of activities and he had grown to rely on her common sense and her continuing presence. Did she know how much she meant to him? Probably not. He knew that he had been taking her for granted for so many years and through so many trials – surely she realised how important she was to the children, to everyone in the house and to him, even though he knew, guiltily, that he had not shown her the appreciation she deserved. Nor had he told her that he loved her. Barnabas put his hands over his face and groaned aloud, frightening Ewella who was just coming in with a jug of cold water as Dr. Trevell had instructed. Barnabas tried to hold Eliza up to sip the water but she just murmured incoherently and turned her head away.

The day passed and dusk drew in. Still Barnabas sat by his wife, ignoring the stiffness in his limbs and refusing to go down for supper. A concerned Caroline brought him a plate of food but it remained untouched and Ewella cleared it away. When she tried to remonstrate with her brother he looked at her with such misery that she knew she must leave him alone. The night passed and still Barnabas maintained his vigil. He moistened her lips with water at intervals and stroked her forehead but she made no sign that she knew he was there. Morning brought Dr. Trevell again. He said Eliza should be washed with cool water and cold flannels left on her brow in an effort to reduce her fever. There was nothing else he could suggest. It was a matter of waiting. Barnabas insisted on doing everything for Eliza himself and banned everyone from the sickroom except for Ewella. Caroline was annoyed but understood that it would help nobody if she succumbed to the 'flu as well.

Grace did not want to see her sister and suggested to Ewella that it would be a good idea if she, Grace, took refuge at the Manor. Coldly Ewella pointed out that there were cases of influenza among the children there and Austol would be kept busy enough without extra guests. So Grace retired to her room and sulked. Far from helping to look after the children she left all of them in Miss Maisie's care.

Selena also was in sulky mood as she wandered round the house without discernible purpose or spent time gazing out of the windows at the sea. Ewella assured the children cheerily that their mother would be better soon. John, Nessa and Joel believed her without question as did Elestren but Richard could not hide the anxiety he felt for his beloved aunt

Edgar was the next visitor to Roscarne, bearing an immense bouquet of flowers from Austol's hot house at the Manor. He reported that the twins were recovering from the influenza but Elowen was still racked by fever and they were all worried about her. Austol was out of his mind that another of his daughters was in danger but still he sent his warmest wishes for Eliza's speedy recovery as did all the other girls.

     'Eliza will not be helping him to look after his family,' Barnabas stated grimly.' She will stay here and look after her own. And I shall look after her!'
Edgar decided not to pass that message on to Austol.

30

Nathaniel was relatively untouched by the furore over the Quinns' departure. As he had been at school they did not figure much in his life. His mother, however, was a different matter. Like Barnabas, he did not expect her to be ill – ever. She was the granite rock round which everything in the house surged and swirled. For her to be seriously ill was cataclysmic. Nathaniel reacted to this by painting ever more furiously. Day after day he took his easel, paints and canvases out and did not reappear until supper time. He did not confine himself to Marah Cove only but wandered further afield, sometimes on the moor, sometimes to Ros Sands, sometimes to Marietta Cove which was closer to home. High winds and rough seas did not deter him; he wanted to paint the coastline in all its moods. In some of his paintings Lamorna still appeared but in others he created fantasy figures which he knew did not conform to the requirements of 'plein air'. And he waited. There had, as yet, been no word from Jean Luc as to how he had fared at the Royal Academy in London. The certainty he had felt, fuelled by Jean Luc's enthusiasm, slowly oozed away.

One summer day of blue skies and bluer sea he received a shock. He was back in Marah Cove trying to catch that particular shade of blue when a figure appeared on the sand – a girl in a white dress with masses of black hair. Lamorna? Of course not. He rubbed his eyes. It was Selena, bored and restive who had followed him, not interested in his paintings but more than interested in the handsome young man with tragic eyes.

'How is my mother? Is she improving at last?' The shock made him speak gruffly.

'Barnabas is still at her side so I am sure she is being well looked after.' There was no concern in her voice, only sarcasm and Nathaniel was repulsed by her cold tones. How could anyone look so attractive and yet have no real warmth or sympathy? Sensing that she had made a bad impression Selena scrambled up the rocks to stand beside him, rather closer than was necessary. She held on to his arm to keep her balance and he could smell her musky scent as she wriggled even closer, pressing her breasts against him, while exclaiming with admiration as she examined his painting.

'That's not a real person.' She pointed to the figure he had sketched in, a figure skeletally thin with straggled hair. 'I know! Why don't you paint me? I am better looking than that creature!'

'That creature, as you call her is meant to be Death! She is not meant to be real.' Nathaniel was glacial. But against his will he was stirred by the warmth of her body so close to his and rather ashamed of his rudeness.

'We can come here again if you wish and I will paint you. But I want to finish this before dusk.' His tone was dismissive and Selena pouted. However Nathaniel had become immersed again in his painting and she could see he had forgotten her so she jumped down from the rocks and wandered off along the beach towards Roscarne.

Back at the house, Eliza's fever had faded and she seemed to be sleeping normally. Barnabas took the opportunity to change his clothes and report on Eliza's progress. Ewella crept into her room to see that she had enough water and found her lying there, her eyes wide open.

'Ewella!' she croaked. 'Have you been with me? I thought it was Seth.' Ewella frowned.

'No, my dear, you have been dreaming! Seth and Rose are far away by now. Barnabas has been at your side for the last three days, hardly moving at all. He's had no food, not

176

much sleep – he has shown real devotion. He is just telling your family that you are on the mend. Now I shall wash you and bring you a fresh nightdress and then you shall have some soup.'

Eliza smiled weakly and tried to absorb what Ewella had said. Seth far away? Barnabas by her side for so long? Gradually the events of the past few weeks came back to her, still with the same old questions. How could Seth leave her? And why was Barnabas still spending so much time with Selena? The problem of Selena had to be resolved. No longer would she put up with a strange woman, not a relation, monopolizing her husband's time. He would have to explain himself. At the thought, Eliza felt exhausted and Barnabas crept back to find her fast asleep.

Slowly Eliza gained back her strength. The children were allowed to come and visit her, each showing their relief in different ways. Joel jumped around her like a firecracker, his red hair on end, and soon earned a rebuke from Ewella. John stood by her bed, straight like a soldier, and spoke very formally about his pleasure that his mother was well again and she should not go outside without a warm shawl as the weather was still uncertain. Eliza smiled and promised she would not do anything so thoughtless. Nessa did not say much but smiled a lot. Caroline, however, worried Eliza. She was so pale and seemed to have lost weight; she admitted to her mother that Nathaniel was causing her extra concern.

'That Selena is always hanging around him,' she complained. 'Even worse, Nathaniel seems to be encouraging her. She follows him wherever he goes and I believe he is actually painting her!'

'Don't forget Nathaniel must still be missing Lamorna,' said her mother, soothingly. 'Perhaps a little female attention will do him good.' Privately she wondered what Barnabas thought but she did not yet feel strong enough to tackle him on the subject. He came to see her every morning before was leaving for Wheal Eliza and there was a kindness and affection in his eyes that she had not seen for a long time. He confined himself to brief enquiries about her health and made little of his vigil as she stammered thanks for his care during her illness.

It was puzzling that there was no sign of Richard. Or Elestren. Grace had put her head round Eliza's door and said she was pleased that her sister was looking better but had not stayed long enough for Eliza to ask where they were. Then one night, just when she had settled to sleep, her door creaked open and Richard crept in.

'Richard! I thought you would be in bed by now! But it is so good to see you!'

'Mama does not know I am here. She said it was too soon to bother you,' confided Richard. 'I have been so miserable without you, but Mama said you were not my mother and you would only want to see your own children just now. But I couldn't wait.'

'You know that you and Elestren are just as precious to me as all the others!' smiled Eliza. 'Usually I would not encourage you to disobey your mother but I think she has just made a mistake.' Inside she was raging at yet another example of Grace's lack of feeling for both her sister and her son.

'Don't worry, I shall ask your mother especially to let you come again. And to bring Elestren with you.' Richard left with a smile on his face.

Finally Eliza left her sickbed for good and was able to wander through her beloved Roscarne and chat to Uncle Tobias and Miss Maisie. She visited Mrs Adwyn in the kitchen and thanked her for the tasty soups she had made and shared a cup of tea and some hevvacake with her.

'That will put flesh on your bones!' said the cook, forgetting that she was talking to the mistress of the house. Eliza just laughed. She went to the schoolroom and inspected the children's books and was particularly delighted to find that Joel had improved so much. No longer was he confined to working on a slate but had an exercise book of his own which, proudly, he showed to his mother. 'Richard helps me sometimes,' he informed Eliza. 'Now I am nearly as good as Nessa and she is older than me.' Nessa just smiled. The only discordant note was her conflict with John. He did not see why he should return to school when Nathaniel was allowed to do as he liked.

'It's not fair! I shall be the only one not at home!' he protested. Eliza knew that she had to stand firm. John was too clever for Miss Maisie, particularly in mathematics and he had been thriving at school. John himself knew that a plea to his father would be useless so resigned himself to another year.

Selena she met by chance in the morning room. Since the girl had become attracted to Nathaniel there had been fewer outings with Barnabas.

'I am pleased to see that you have recovered,' said Selena, her polite words at odds with the defiant look in her eyes. Eliza smiled as sincerely as she could manage. Encouraged, Selena rushed on: 'I was hoping to catch Nathaniel but I can't find him – Barnabas, I mean Mr. Barnabas wants me to go to Camborne today but I'm so tired of looking – ' she stopped, confused.

'Looking for what?' asked Eliza. Selena cast about her wildly, seeking an escape.

'Why Camborne?'

'There's a big fair there,' she blurted and edged round Eliza as if she were contaminated and darted through the door.

31

Eliza sat in her attic room and stared out of the window. The sea and sky were vying with each other in their shades of blue but for once she did not notice. She was musing over Barnabas. They had grown closer to each other since her illness; they had been able to discuss the children quite amiably and Barnabas made a point of keeping Eliza abreast of mining matters. But, like a boulder on a cliff path, Selena stood in their way. Why did her husband want to take Selena to a fair in Camborne? It was important enough for him to growl at her when she put in a late appearance, resulting in her flouncing off, shaking her black hair in defiance.

'I don't want to come today. Nathaniel said he was going to paint me!'

'This is all for your benefit! I am unable to take you for the rest of the week!' But Selena had gone. Barnabas turned to Eliza in despair.

'What shall I do?' he groaned.

'It would help if you explained to me why Selena is here at all!' said Eliza, acidly. 'Why are you squiring her to so many places? Why is she so important to you?' She took a deep breath.' Are you in love with her?'

Barnabas looked flabbergasted. 'ME? In love with Selena? You must be out of your mind. I am trying to get rid of the silly woman! She made me promise not to tell anyone at all what this is all about but surely, Eliza, you should know me better than to imagine I was in love with her!' Eliza realised that her husband was full of indignation, emphatic enough to be righteous, his face drained of colour.

'Then, Barnabas, you should explain to me – never mind if you break a promise to her. I am more important to you I hope!'

They sat together in the morning room and Barnabas took her hands in his.

'I am really hurt that you should entertain such ideas about me. I thought you trusted me.'

'Remember Grace? That shook my faith in you even though you tried to explain it away.'

Barnabas shifted uncomfortably in his chair. 'That was such a long time ago. I did try to make it clear what had happened and why.'

'It gave me such a shock at the time!'

'Look what you put me through when you ran away,' he countered. They stared at each other, remembering difficult times in the past.

'Now,' said Eliza. 'Please tell me. I have let things slide long enough.'

'You had other concerns all last year, I believe?'

Eliza felt her face redden. 'What do you mean?'

'Seth.' The name dropped like a stone in a pool. 'You were so agitated about them coming to stay with us even though Rose was your best friend. Then the tension between the two of you was hard to ignore sometimes.'

'Why – why did you not say anything?' faltered Eliza.

'Because I trusted you both. I expected that it would all die a natural death, anyway. There was no future in it. However it was Rose who determined to take her husband out of harm's way!'

Eliza could have sworn that there was a twinkle in her husband's eye. It was then she realised that Barnabas had a confidence in their marriage that no one could shatter.

At this propitious moment in bustled Ewella announcing that Austol had come to call. With him, rather unusually, was Kenwyn.

'Show him into the drawing room and I shall be along directly,' said Barnabas.

'I believe he is here to see Mistress Eliza,' said Ewella, never one to avoid a chance of fomenting trouble. To be fair to her, she resented Austol and his attempts to build a friendship with her brother's wife, however innocent. 'Oh – and Mr. Kenwyn is here to see Miss Caroline. Apparently she is expecting him.'

'Eliza, I shall inform Austol that you are unavailable,' Barnabas said firmly. But Eliza was not to be superseded so easily.

'I shall accompany you, Barnabas,' she said sweetly. 'Obviously Austol has something to say to me. I did not know that Kenwyn had some arrangement with Caroline but I shall fetch her. Then afterwards we shall continue our conversation about Selena.' She rose. 'We had better not keep him waiting,' she said and left the room, followed by an outflanked Barnabas.

If Austol was surprised to see both of them, he did not show it. Eliza, however, was astonished to see an Austol restored to himself, with little sign of the dreadful grief he had suffered. He was cheery and in the grip of a particular excitement.

'Mistress Eliza, you are aware that I destroyed so many of Lamorna's paintings,' he began. 'Now, some time on, I bitterly regret having done so. But an idea has come to me.' He paused. 'I intend to open a gallery in Truro. The gallery will show paintings based in Cornwall, paintings of our time executed by our artists and it will be a memorial to Lamorna.' He sat back in his chair, obviously pleased with his own idea. Barnabas spoke first. 'This is good news indeed – but in what way can we help you?'

Austol leaned forward, speaking with an intensity he could not hide.

'I need help from your Nathaniel and I need your permission to ask him. I have been in touch with Jean Luc who tells me that your son has an artistic talent, rare in one who has had no formal tuition. Lamorna attempted to tell me the same thing but I was too stubborn to listen.'

'How do you want Nathaniel to help you?' asked Eliza.

'In two ways. I should so like him to paint Lamorna again. That, of course, is most important.'

'I thought you were so angry with Nathaniel,' interrupted Eliza, unable to believe in this complete change of attitude.

'The grief I felt in losing Lamorna made me unreasonable in many ways. Edgar tells me that I have been very difficult for some time.' Austol managed a sheepish smile. 'I now realise that what happened was a terrible accident and no one's fault. I feel I have been so unfair to Nathaniel and I should like to make it up to him. I hope that he can repeat some of the portraits he did of her.'

'And the second way?' Barnabas said. Austol looked uncomfortable.

'I do not know if you are both aware that I have been married twice?' Eliza nodded but Barnabas, surprised, shook his head. 'My first wife, Jenifer, was very dear to me. I should so much like to have a portrait of her but I destroyed it. Now Mistress Eliza is very like her. In fact the resemblance is quite remarkable. It was Edgar who pointed that out to me. I thought perhaps Nathaniel could paint you, Mistress Eliza, in a setting where I remember Jenifer, and that would go some way towards restoring her to me.' Austol stood up and spoke more gently, looking down at his listeners who were both moved by his words.

'Losing Lamorna has made me realise that my family is important to me, more important than being Lord of the Manor, more important than money. Jenifer was dear to me in a way I never recognised while I was indulging in worthless pursuits, chasing recognition from my peers and losing my temper when the world did not spin my way.' He turned for the door. 'I know that you will need some time to think over what I have just said. Please stay where you are. Ewella will see me out.' He left before Eliza or Barnabas could utter a word.

'Well, Eliza, what do you think of Austol's proposition?'
'We can ask Nathaniel and see what he says.'
'I should value your opinion on this matter.'
Eliza raised her eyebrows at her husband. He was not in the habit of asking for her opinion about anything and when she did offer unsolicited observations about a matter, he tended to ignore her.
'I cannot imagine anything worse than losing a child,' she said firmly. 'Because of this I feel very sorry for Austol even though I – I do not like him very much. I think we should ask Nathaniel if he would be willing to paint Lamorna again – it would have to be from memory and that would stir up his feelings of grief so he may have strong opinions about that. As for painting me – I am sure that my son would willingly paint his mother.' She continued innocently, 'But then did I understand you to say that my portrait should not hang at the Manor – not ever?'
Barnabas looked at her closely. Was Eliza teasing him?
'If you are supposed to be Jenifer then that is something different,' he declared.

32

Nathaniel came in late for supper. He was soaked to the skin from the light but persistent summer drizzle and Eliza insisted he should change at once.

'I do not know how you can paint when the weather is like this!' she scolded.

'I have an umbrella for my easel,' said Nathaniel. 'The weather helps to create a mood for my paintings. It would be boring if it was sunny every day.'

'That is so true,' said Selena, eagerly. 'I should love to see a real storm with howling winds and huge waves. But you could not paint then, Nathaniel, could you?'

'Yes he could,' said an ever supportive Caroline.

'It depends,' said Nathaniel.

Barnabas looked at his son with new interest. How he had grown up in the last few difficult months. When he had worked through his obsession with painting perhaps he would be mature enough to take over from Seth at Wheal Rose – so ran his thoughts. Fortunately he did not hint at this to Nathaniel; the resultant row would have split the family again. Nathaniel had shown no interest in mining, a fact even Uncle Tobias had observed.

'Your mother and I wish to speak with you, Nathaniel. Please come into the drawing room when you have finished your supper.' Nathaniel looked on the verge of protesting but Caroline gave him a warning push.

'It won't be anything bad,' she whispered. 'They have to be kind to you for a long time yet!' Her brother gave her a wan smile as she hurried off to see Kenwyn who was waiting patiently in the hallway.

'How you paint Lamorna is up to you,' said Austol, standing in front of the unused fireplace, his arms clasped behind his back. 'I have explained to your mother and father how deeply I regret destroying so many paintings. Jean Luc saved some of them but I should value one of Lamorna, especially when executed by someone who was close to her and appreciated her many qualities. Are your memories of her clear enough to allow you to paint her?'

'Oh yes,' replied Nathaniel. He looked Austol straight in the face. 'I shall never forget her. And my depiction of her will ensure that you remember her also.'

'Where will you do your painting?'

'I know where but the weather must be right.' Nathaniel refused to say more.

'Now – your mother. I thought perhaps you could – '

'No. Please allow me to decide what to do – ' Austol looked irritated. Nathaniel was argumentative like his mother.

'I want her to look like my first wife, Jenifer – '

'I know that,' said Nathaniel. 'And I know Lamorna was her daughter. So I believe like mother, like daughter. Edgar tells me – '

'Edgar?!'

'I have done some research in order to do the best I can. Edgar has been very helpful. If you do not agree with what I decide then perhaps Jean Luc could find someone else who – '

'NO! You are close to your mother and close to Lamorna. I leave it to you.'

'Thank you.'

Meanwhile a disconsolate Selena found she could not engage the attention of either Barnabas or Nathaniel and ended up complaining to Grace who was having a late cup of coffee in the morning room.

'I do not understand why you bother with either of them,' said Grace, disparagingly. 'Barnabas is rooted here in

Roscarne and Nathaniel has no money. If I were you I should try for Austol – or even Edgar.'

'They are both too old,' scowled Selena. 'Besides I am not looking for a husband. I am looking for – 'she stopped.

'What ARE you looking for?' queried Grace. Selena put her hand over her mouth. 'I cannot tell you. It is a secret. Only Barnabas knows and he is not allowed to tell Eliza or anyone else.'

Grace was going through one of her sharper times and Selena intrigued her. One minute she was arrogantly flaunting new clothes around the house, the next she was playing the part of a poor little lost girl. With her thick black hair, flashing eyes and undoubted beauty this latter role did not suit her. What was going on? However Selena realized that she had been on the verge of saying too much. She made her excuses and went to see Mrs. Adwyn in the kitchen instead. Grace shrugged her shoulders and promptly forgot her.

'Nathaniel, where are you going to paint me?' asked Eliza. 'Inside or outdoors?' She was slightly in awe of this handsome young man, considered by some to be a talented artist, yet still her son, her first born.

'Mama, your turn will come. I need to think about this some more. Meanwhile I shall paint Lamorna while she is still in my memory.' He did not wince or show any sign that the prospect was at all daunting or sad. He refused to say more and Eliza had to be content. When Uncle Tobias heard what was going on, he spluttered with indignation.

'It is impossible!' he declared. 'Eliza should not be a model for Austol's first wife! What will other people think! And poor Lamorna! She should be allowed to rest in peace.'

Grace heard this outburst and nodded her head sagely. Of course Uncle Tobias was right.

Barnabas felt that nothing more was required of him after his meeting with Austol and Eliza learned from Ewella that he had taken Selena to Camborne. Eliza felt that news like a slap.

She and Barnabas had grown so much closer and now he was back taking Selena here, there and everywhere – or at least to Camborne. She gritted her teeth. He would have to explain himself. The situation turned out quite differently when Barnabas returned. He bounded up to the attic room, flung the door open and whirled Eliza round in a wild waltz.

'Selena has found him! She's found him!' he cried exultantly.

'Found him? Who?'

'I can tell you, now! You will not be bothered with her any longer!'

'Just tell me calmly what has happened!' demanded Eliza.

'We have been looking for Selena's brother.'

'I thought she had no family left after her mother died?'

'The brother was never mentioned when I was there. He was serving a long prison sentence when I was staying with them and of course Selena did not want anyone else to know. It was bad enough for her reputation to have a father in prison – but a brother as well!' Barnabas eyed Eliza to see if she was taking all this in and was relieved to see that she looked interested but not censorious. He continued 'Selena decided that she would like to find him – I believe she thought that he would look after her. As you might have noticed she is not keen to work, to find employment of any kind. However, when we did try to see him at the prison in Exeter we found that he had finished his prison term and was free. But we could not find him. We have been to every fair, market, agricultural show in this part of Cornwall because Selena was sure that was where he would be, looking for work. And we found him at last at Camborne fair!'

Before Eliza could utter a word, the door opened and Caroline rushed in. Barnabas was about to reprove her but Eliza put her finger to her lips. Abashed, Barnabas sat back. Now what?

'Mama, Kenwyn would like to take me out for a ride in his pony and trap! May I go? Please say yes, the sun is shining and I believe spring has come at last!'
Again Barnabas endeavoured to respond but Eliza beat him to it.

'What a good idea,' she smiled. 'I can see no reason why not. Kenwyn is a nice young man and it will be good to talk on different subjects!'

'Papa?' Caroline remembered her manners and turned to her father. Barnabas managed a smile of approval but then added 'And who is to be your chaperone?'

'Miss Maisie! She said a dose of fresh air is just what she needs!' Caroline skipped off.

'That is the happiest I have seen her for a long while,' her father commented. 'Eliza, I do believe you have been plotting this!'
Eliza smiled complacently.

'It was not good for her to be so attached to Nathaniel that his problems became hers. She has to lead her own life even if she is a twin. Austol has not been a particularly good father to Kenwyn and this will give him a new dimension in his life.'

'I have never thought of our daughter as a dimension!'

33

'Is that all? That is your big secret? Why on earth did Selena want to keep that so quiet?' Eliza was puzzled. All the time she had spent worrying just for this.

'See it from her point of view. Her father had been in prison and her brother still was at the time her mother died. Not a recommendation for employment. When we went to Falmouth we found that her brother had been released and was thought to be wandering the district looking for casual work. We finally caught up with him at Camborne as you know.'

'H'm. So you put me through all that uncertainty just for that! How do you think I felt when you were constantly ferrying Selena to different places!'

'I did not realise at first that you were even concerned! I knew you were not keen on employing another maid so we started searching for Jago – that's her brother, in earnest. And now we have found him and he can take charge of his sister and she does not have to rely on me.'

With the complacent look of one who has untied a particularly intricate knot, Barnabas sprawled on the attic room bed. Eliza looked at him, uncertain whether to be cross or relieved.

'Now, come here, wife. I deserve a little attention do I not?' he patted the bed invitingly.

Later, the two of them, rather ruffled, and Eliza pink faced, descended the stairs to find they had missed lunch.

'Where have you been?' demanded Ewella, as usual forgetting that her brother was master of the house. 'Mrs. Adwyn made a superb herby pie which you have missed.'

'I think Mrs. Adwyn might just be kind enough to serve us whatever is left. We are rather hungry!' Barnabas declared. Uncle Tobias smiled.

The pie was certainly a success. Eliza and Barnabas decided to eat it in the kitchen and were able to praise Mrs. Adwyn's cooking to her face. She was delighted and insisted that they should try her stewed apples for pudding. Then, tactfully, she left them to busy herself in the still room.

'Eliza, I must go and check with Mathey,' said Barnabas when he could eat no more. 'Trembles is lame and I need to see if we should call the animal doctor again.' He bent and kissed his wife's cheek and Eliza felt that a great burden had been lifted from her shoulders. Selena was not a threat and never had been. It dawned on her that thoughts of Seth had not crossed her mind for some hours – after all he was so very far away. And Rose? If she were totally honest she would admit that she would have done the same thing as had Rose. She and Seth together generated such vibrations that it had been clever of her friend to remove her husband from temptation.

The next morning was dark, threatening rain. Large black clouds were rolling in and the wind was rising. Everyone in Roscarne could hear the booming as the waves of the incoming tide broke against the foot of the cliffs and echoed in the caves. Barnabas had left early to fetch the animal doctor and Caroline was in the stables comforting the fretful pony. Grace had not yet put in an appearance, nor had Uncle Tobias. Miss Maisie however was anxious to begin lessons and marshalled the children into the schoolroom. Eliza, feeling an unaccustomed languor, decided to creep up to the attic and watch the sea from there. There was no sign of Nathaniel.

It was Caroline, always uneasy on stormy days, who wanted to find her brother. She crept into his room when there was no answer to her knocking and saw he was not there; with dread weighing down her spirits she went to find Eliza. This was easier. She was in the morning room, mending a dress belonging to Nessa and bemoaning the fact that it was so dark. Conscience had brought her down from the attic, the feeling that she was allowing such tasks to mount up.

'Those heavy curtains make it so dark in here, even when the sun is shining,' she said crossly. 'As it is, with this weather, I cannot even see white stitching, never mind black – Caroline? What is the matter?'

'It's Nathaniel! He does not seem to be in the house!'

'I am sure he is – somewhere,' said her mother, reassuringly. 'He would not be out on a day like this.' She stopped. Of course he would. The weather would not stop him. Not Nathaniel.

'Don't look so worried, Caroline. After what happened he will take care – in any case the tide must be ebbing by now.' She jumped up, suddenly alarmed by the look on Caroline's face. 'Surely he would not go painting – ? But we had better look.' So Eliza and Caroline, swathed in oilskins, ventured down the path to Marietta Cove. The howling of the wind could only just be heard above the crash of heavy breakers exploding in shards of white on the rocks.

'He prefers Marah Cove!' shouted Caroline above the noise of wind and sea. Heads down, they tramped across the sand and round the next promontory to Marah Cove. The ebbing tide had left a tract of wet sand before the rocks and the angry waves. No footsteps marred its pristine surface.

'He's not here!' shouted Caroline. Eliza nodded. Glad to get away from sad memories they hurried on, aiming for Ros Sands. Then Eliza stopped and listened.

'There IS someone in Marah Cove. I heard shouting. It must be Nathaniel.' They turned back. There was the cluster of rocks where Nathaniel and Lamorna had been painting that dreadful day, rocks blackened by the tides, rearing up like giant's teeth while water smacked over them. Every now and again a wave broke free and rushed up the beach against the pull of the tide and Caroline shuddered. They looked like predators hunting a victim. They looked hungry.

'What ARE you two doing here?'
Through the rain, now lancing down, a figure appeared. It was Nathaniel.

'Oh Nathaniel, we were searching for you!' Caroline flung her arms around him. Eliza relaxed in her relief and managed a smile even though rain was dripping down her neck and off the end of her nose. Nathaniel looked from one to the other.

'Surely you did not think I was going to follow Lamorna and drown myself!' He pushed back his hair which hung in lank strands over his face. 'I am here to absorb the atmosphere and plan how I am going to paint her but the rain was so heavy I had to shelter in a cave – that one just behind you. Now I shall have to escort you two back to the house.' He grinned at them cheerfully. 'Perhaps Mrs. Adwyn will heat up some of her cinnamon scones for us, we look pathetic enough.'

The three of them trudged over wet sand and through standing water to reach the path up to Roscarne. Eliza was glad to leave Marah Cove. The wind and rain were bad enough but there was an extra chill there, generated she was sure, by the previous tragedy. It needed sunny days and passing time to allow the sad memories to evaporate and vanish in spindrift and spray.

Back at Roscarne they were surprised to be met by Ewella at the door.

'A visitor!' she hissed. 'Wants to see Nathaniel! Thank goodness you found him.'

'Who is it?' Ewella shrugged. 'We must put on dry clothes,' instructed Eliza. 'All three of us look like tramps. Please offer the visitor some tea, Ewella, and we shall be down directly.' Ewella looked as if she wanted to run away but she took a deep breath and re-entered the drawing room. Eliza was the first to come down and face the visitor. It was Jean Luc. He had exchanged his painter's smock for a jacket of ginger brown tweed and looked smarter than usual. He stood up as she entered and smiled widely.

'Ah, Mistress Trevannion! I 'ave grand plaisir in seeing you today. How are you after these sad times? 'Ow is Nathaniel? And where is he? Mistress Ewella said he was just coming back from the beach? On a day comme ca?'

'He will be down in a moment,' said Eliza. 'He told us he was absorbing the atmosphere for a painting he wishes to do but we feared he was lost – '

At this point Nathaniel entered. His face lit up to see Jean Luc.

'I have news for you,' said Jean Luc gravely. Nathaniel held his breath.

'I took your painting of Lamorna to the Royal Academy as I promised.'

'Yes?' Nathaniel could only whisper.

'And they will hang it in the Summer Exhibition!'

34

Nathaniel took a deep breath. This was not his first visit to the Manor but at least for once he had been invited. He waited in the hall while the maid went to announce him to Austol and in the intervening time he glanced around. He could see that the Manor was entirely different in concept from Roscarne. The floor was polished to a high gloss, a fine woven rug, probably Turkish, lay in front of the empty fireplace, a large gold framed mirror adorned one wall and an oil painting of, presumably, a Treloyhan ancestor, glowered down from the other. And this was just the hallway. Here, at the Manor he knew, Lamorna had felt she was in a prison in spite of the undoubted luxury of her home and her father had been her prison warder. Yet Austol had mourned for his daughter to the extent of becoming ill and having a near break down – or so Ewella told him. Now Austol wanted him to capture the essence of his first wife, Jenifer, by painting Eliza who, apparently looked so like her. Nathaniel could not believe that his father would agree to such a mad scheme. But he had.

'He feels that we should do anything we can to help Austol,' explained Eliza. 'And I feel the same. We are lucky that you are here but he has lost Lamorna –'
Nathaniel knew that they still felt he was indirectly responsible for her death. So he was but he had not ignited the desire to paint in Lamorna – if anything she had encouraged him.

'This way, sir.' The maid led him down a wide corridor to Austol's study. And there he was, face to face again with Lamorna's father.

Austol was a surprise. Nathaniel had expected him to be still wan and sickly but in fact he radiated energy and purpose. He was immaculate in white frilled shirt, well-polished black boots, oiled whiskers and his hair smoothed back with macassar oil. Still a handsome man in spite of the heavy lines the events of the last few months had exaggerated on his face.

'Mistress Eliza? I expected her to accompany you?' His disappointment was plain.

'My mother had another engagement but she sends her best wishes and is happy to agree with whatever we decide,' said Nathaniel politely. 'I do have some good news for you. At least I hope you will be pleased.'

'Go on.'

'Jean Luc tells me that my painting of Lamorna is to be hung in the Summer Exhibition at the Royal Academy.' There was a silence. Anxiously Nathaniel waited. Austol summoned a smile.

'You must be talented, my boy. I am pleased to hear of your success.'

'Also I have nearly finished a similar one of Lamorna for you to have.'

'And some happier ones to come, I hope.'

'Oh yes.'

Austol changed the subject.

'I should like Mistress Eliza to wear this dress – fortunately I kept some of Jenifer's things – and a pearl necklace that she was fond of and wore often. The background is your choice.'

'I should like to do one of her in Marah Cove where her daughter died – but I should also like to do one here at the Manor.'

'I am pleased that you will do more than one,' said Austol, 'I like to think of Jenifer and Lamorna together but I shall appreciate one in happier surroundings.'

Nathaniel smiled in relief. He had expected some opposition.

'Lord Treloyhan, if painting from memory is successful I should be willing to do more,' he said eagerly. Austol smiled at him, a smile that came more easily. He was beginning to see why his daughter had been so attracted to this boy. Furthermore he might well achieve what he had desired in the first instance – a painting of Mistress Eliza.

'I think we should drink to our agreement,' said Austol. 'But it should be coffee.' Nathaniel's disappointment showed.

Back at Roscarne and breathless with excitement Nathaniel held up the blue velvet dress to Eliza's critical gaze.

'It looks like my size except the neckline is all wrong,' conceded Eliza. 'I will ask Grace if she can help me. She sews well when she wants to. And what have you there?'

'A necklace of Jenifer's that Austol would like you to wear.' He opened the box he was carrying and showed the collar of matching pearls, pearls which glowed with a quiet lustre. Eliza gasped. She had never before seen such a necklace, let alone worn one.

'Mama, if I am a success as an artist, I shall buy you pearls just like that,' Nathaniel assured her. 'Let us take care we do not lose those in the meantime. Lock them up in my bureau.' was his mother's tart rejoinder.

'We need to wait for a calm day,' said Nathaniel. 'I don't want another stormy picture and I don't want to put you at risk.' Eliza smiled at him. She was proud of her son and was sure that all the blame was not attributable to him, whatever Austol thought. Capricious Lamorna had led the way to London, then deserted him for someone else. Then her son had compensated by becoming engrossed in the painting he was doing

The calm day they wished for finally arrived. They woke to a pale grey day. The sky was overcast and the sea still as glass.

'Now we can start!' Nathaniel was exultant. He collected his easel, a new fold up easel Jean Luc had given him, and his paints and palette. Eliza, his model, followed him in her blue dress and pearls. They had intended to slide out without disturbing anyone but as luck would have it, Barnabas caught them. The sight of Eliza in her blue velvet riveted him. How beautiful she was still, her dark hair without grey and her complexion glowing with reflected light from the pearls. He smiled at her with pride.

'Nathaniel, please take care. I know the tide should be receding just now – '

'Papa, do not worry. I shall take care of her.'

Barnabas believed his son, but some sixth sense stopped him from leaving Roscarne for Wheal Rose as he had intended. He headed for his study but found he could not settle to the paperwork that awaited him so he sank into an easy chair and lit a cigar.

The reasons for his unease slipped and scrambled down the cliff path to Marietta Cove, Eliza taking care of her velvet dress by hiking it up and showing much of her chemise; then they walked on to Marah Cove which was also deserted. The tide was still ebbing and each new wave broke listlessly on the sand then withdrew without vigour.

'Mama, I should like you to stand on that plateau of granite with the sea as your background. I shall paint you, leaning against a rock and gazing out to sea as if you are waiting for someone to return.'

'No acting needed,' thought Eliza. 'I shall just think of Seth.' The look on her face pleased Nathaniel and he began to sketch with fervour. His concentration was intense and Eliza was determined not to interrupt him so she fell into a daydream during which she had some difficulty involving Seth as Barnabas was always there. Neither artist nor model paid any heed to the tide.

After an hour or more Eliza groaned and asked for a change of position. It was then they realized that something strange had happened. The slowly ebbing tide had gathered speed and was already further out than usual. A strong smell of seaweed tainted the air. In the rockpools the water glinted like metal and the rocks revealed by the tide appeared dark with running moisture. A strange silence hung over the bay, intensified as no gulls were flying.

35

Meanwhile Caroline and Kenwyn had abandoned outings with the pony and trap and Miss Maisie and decided to walk instead. Miss Maisie was delighted as she did not enjoy being a third person and the task was taking up her spare time. Caroline and Kenwyn were also constrained in their conversation and found they were skimming the surface of communication which was most unsatisfactory. Caroline in particular wanted to know much more of Kenwyn's relationship with his father. Then he had pretended to be a deserter from the army. Why? Kenwyn, in turn, was curious about Barnabas and why Eliza felt the need to help out Austol so often. He had heard whispers about his uncle, Sir James, and Grace, Mistress Eliza's sister and was curious to know what had happened all those years ago.

They walked round the rhododendron gardens at first and then decided to venture further as no one had challenged them. Caroline had an uneasy feeling that she should have asked permission but Kenwyn had no such scruples.
   'It is so old fashioned to have a chaperone,' he complained, 'Even such a retiring one as Miss Maisie. We shall go down the cliff path to the shore and walk by the sea. That would be more – er – desirable, Miss Caroline?'
Caroline nodded. She did not want to confess that walking by the sea was not one of her favourite pastimes any more. Kenwyn did not seem at all concerned that his sister had met her death so close by and she did not think it politic to remind him. However he surprised her by remarking that the living should not allow the dead to dictate their actions as if he had known what she was thinking.

Carefully they negotiated the cliff path, Kenwyn steadying Caroline by holding her arm which she found quite exciting. Then he gave an exclamation.

'There has been a cliff fall – quite a considerable one!'

'Do you know what caused it?' Caroline shook her head.

'Maybe the rain, maybe a slight earthquake, no one really knows.' They resumed their leisurely stroll once they reached the beach of Marietta Cove. Caroline liked walking with Kenwyn. He adjusted his steps to match hers and guided her around the seaweed left by the tide. And he could discuss so many ideas, so many subjects, asking for her opinion on various topics. So unlike Nathaniel who seemed full of his own concerns or totally silent. But he had been so involved with Lamorna that to lose her must have been a terrible shock. Then enthusiasm for his painting had taken him over and he seemed to have no time to spare for his twin. She stole a look at the young man by her side. He was so handsome. His back was ramrod straight, his features as if carved from rock. His eyes, a warm brown, looked at her with interest and Caroline was completely won over. She shivered when he held her hand and wondered if this was what Nathaniel had felt for Lamorna.

Suddenly, Kenwyn gave an exclamation.

'Look at the tide! It seems extremely far out.'

Caroline looked doubtful. 'A spring tide I expect but I have never seen it as low as this.' They stared at the expanse of sand and rocks revealed by the tide, a tide which was so far out that it seemed to reach the horizon. The unexpected vista made Caroline feel strange. All that water. When would it return? Kenwyn had the same thought.

'I think we should get back. I should like to find out more about spring tides. Perhaps your father or your Uncle Tobias might have some information.' Caroline was not listening. A sudden fear had gripped her. Where was

Nathaniel? And Eliza? Had he chosen this calm grey day to paint her?

'Kenwyn, do you think we could go on to Marah Cove? It may be that Nathaniel is painting there and –'

'Absolutely not!' said Kenwyn firmly. 'We need to return to Roscarne first and find out more.' He would listen to no more argument but, holding Caroline firmly by the arm, marched her back to Marietta Cove and the cliff path to Roscarne.

'What on earth has happened? The tide does not usually go out so far?' Eliza was intrigued, not yet nervous.

'I don't know. I think it may be to do with the spring. We always have higher and lower tides then.' Nathaniel was abstracted, anxious to continue painting and no freak of nature was going to disturb him.

'Mama – if you could resume your position I can continue?'

'Nathaniel?'

'There is nothing we can do about it,' said Nathaniel so, uneasily, Eliza took up her stance leaning against the rock. Her mind wandered to her family. Uncle Tobias seemed to have shaken off his succession of colds with the help of the early spring warmth and it was to be hoped that the return of winter would not affect him as much as the previous year.

Then there was Grace, still veering from normality to a strange state of uncertain moods and exaggerated tempers. She was no worse than she had been for the last year but her instability was always a cause for anxiety especially with regard to the children, Richard and Elestren. Richard. What a lovely boy he was and how bravely he managed his mother when she was distressed. Elestren however was not easy to fathom. She was a pretty blonde child with an elfin face; she could laugh and play with the others but sometimes she would retreat into silence and talk to no one, particularly not her mother. Caroline had retreated into herself just recently and confided nothing. Eliza felt sure this was to do with Kenwyn and she wondered how that friendship was progressing. She decided some pertinent questioning was in order, particularly as Caroline was not yet sixteen. Her beloved Caroline, with a touch of the fey about her and a sensitivity towards others, a recognition of feelings deeper than the obvious but also with an accompanying fragility of her own. Her daughter could easily be hurt. And Nessa. Placid, usually smiling and happy, she presented the fewest problems. Even Joel, red haired, fiery, mischievous, rarely teased Nessa and was quick to defend her if someone else did. John? He seemed to Eliza to have been drawn away from his family by the strings of school. He was jealous of the older twins and often felt left out when he was at home. Nathaniel and Caroline were so lucky to have each other he grumbled. Why was he not born a twin? Which made Eliza laugh. Two like John would have been a trial indeed. As a toddler he had been master of some earth shaking tantrums and now, at fifteen years old, he could descend into the depths of gloom and no one could persuade him out of them.

She glanced at Nathaniel, who was concentrating, his forehead furrowed, and decided that she could never be the patient model he needed. He had hardly spoken to her except to admonish her for changing her position and she was bored. Then unexpected movement caught her eye and she forgot her promise to remain still.

'Nathaniel – look!' Nathaniel looked and he, too, was riveted by what he saw. The tide, having receded further than usual, was flooding back, quietly, determinedly and at an unusual speed. There was no wind and the sea appeared the same pearly grey, still flat calm, no waves, but there was an impression of movement below the surface. As they looked the first surge of water reached their granite plateau and swirled silently around it, the levels rising visibly as they watched, horrified. Having surrounded the plateau and the other rocks so recently exposed, the tide waters advanced stealthily across the sand.

'Nathaniel, we must leave at once or we shall be completely cut off! This tide will reach Marah Cliffs very soon. Look at the speed!'

'I am looking!' said Nathaniel irritably. 'Now tell me how we can leave this rock with my painting, my easel, my palette. The water must be six feet deep already!'

'Then soon it will be high enough to cover all of these rocks and the plateau!' Eliza's voice quavered. As she spoke the level of water around them rose further, pushing Nathaniel into action. He rolled up his painting decisively. 'We must paddle through to the sand and leave the Cove by the cliff path. It is the only way. I must keep my painting dry whatever happens. The easel I can fold up with the palette but the painting! That's the real worry!'

'The real worry is for us to reach the safety of Marah Cliffs!' snapped Eliza, angered by his preoccupation with his canvas and his inability to realize that they should act quickly. Nathaniel glanced at her in surprise. It was not like his mother to become so agitated.

'Then we shall have to get wet. I am so sorry, Mama. I should have been paying attention. I really do not know what is happening with the tides – this is not normal.'

Nathaniel lowered himself gingerly over the edge of the rock hanging on by one hand and holding his painting over his head by the other. 'You must follow me, Mama.' He let go of the rock but found to his horror that the current below the surface of the water stopped him just walking. Never a good swimmer he splashed wildly as the water bore him inexorably away from the plateau; at least he still had his painting, Eliza realized, but he had abandoned his new easel and palette. She watched helplessly as his head grew smaller in the distance then she saw him make a wild grab for another rock which had not yet been covered by the water. It would only be a temporary respite but he was looking back to see what Eliza was doing. There was no point in following Nathaniel and it dawned on Eliza that she was in real danger. If he could make little progress in the grip of the current, what hope had she? Such a strong current could strand her on another rock like so much flotsam and damage her in the process. It would be safer to stay where she was and hope the rock she was clinging to would not be completely covered before she could be rescued. Rescue? There was no one in the vicinity and there had not been earlier. There seemed to be a blight on Marah Cove. Those who came down to the shore preferred Ros Sands or pretty Marietta Cove.

Eliza realized the true extent of her predicament as she looked round wildly and began to scream. Perhaps someone would hear her? Perhaps Nathaniel would reach the cliffs and be able to summon help? But where was Nathaniel? She could not see him at all. Was he still clinging to the other side of the rock or had he been washed off? Surely this was a nightmare and she would awaken soon. The slap of water over her feet startled her even more. The water was still rising and her danger was acute. She began to scream again, screamed until she was hoarse and was about to collapse in hopeless tears when, faintly, she thought she heard an answering shout. Distant though it was, she knew that voice. It was Barnabas. She was safe. At last there was the prospect of rescue. A feeling of peace and tranquillity enveloped her, a feeling hardly warranted by her present plight. But Barnabas was strong and he would save them. Her faith in her husband had wavered at times but had always had been there in spite of their clashes and quarrels through the years. Even the time at Carnglaze had not destroyed that faith. The thought flashed through her mind:

'I have to be marooned on a rock, in danger of drowning, to realize that!'

She watched anxiously as Barnabas strode into the water and began to swim towards her. Surely he was making slow progress? He did not seem to be getting any nearer. At this rate she would be washed off the plateau before he could reach her. She would never be able to fight the strength of this strange tide herself and Barnabas was her only hope. And where was Nathaniel? Was he able to see where their son was? Her certainty that they would both be rescued began to falter. Then she heard a shout and two figures appeared on the narrow stretch of sand before the cliffs. Distant though he was she recognized Edgar and with him, Kenwyn. Good. More men to help. Barnabas kept swimming without turning his head and gradually, as he approached, she could see his face contorted with the effort he was making. At last he reached her rock and hung on, water washing over him and pulling at him. He lacked the strength to climb up beside her.

'Eliza, I'm going to swim back – hang on to my leather belt and that will help you.'

'But you need to rest first!'

'I have to keep going! The current should help us towards the shore but when this surge reaches Marah Cliffs it may rebound and it will be too strong for me to battle. Come quickly, Eliza!' She lowered herself into the water feeling the strength of this strange cold tide, a living creature without mercy trying to swallow both of them.

Eliza closed her eyes to stop the splashes of salt water making her eyes sting and to avoid seeing how slowly they were moving. Barnabas was tiring, the water was icy and she was an added weight. She grasped the leather belt hoping frantically that it would not slide through her almost numb fingers.

Then she was pulled on to sand by Edgar, helped by Kenwyn and she and Barnabas lay side by side breathing heavily. Then she sat up in fright. 'Nathaniel! Where is Nathaniel!'

'Here, Mama!' Nathaniel appeared in her line of vision, soaking wet but apparently unharmed. 'Mama – I could not keep the painting from getting wet.' He sounded despairing.

'Goodness, Nathaniel, I shall just have to sit for you again – but somewhere dry this time,' said his mother. Edgar interrupted them.

'We must get to the coast path on Marah Cliffs or we are in danger of getting VERY wet again.' He helped Eliza to her feet while Nathaniel and Kenwyn gave support to Barnabas who was in a state of exhaustion. They staggered towards the entrance to the coast path but the water advanced on them, still with that unexpected strength and cut off their escape.

'Follow me!' said Barnabas, revived by the new danger. 'We shall have to climb the cliffs! There is no way we can reach the path.' He began to scramble up the nearest crag, turning to help Eliza, closely followed by Edgar and Nathaniel with Kenwyn bringing up the rear. The first part was easy, though they loosed stones and earth which tumbled down after their passage. The next slope was steeper and culminated in a fearsome looking overhang before the summit could be reached. Thanks to Barnabas, who remembered some of his boyhood skills in climbing, they at last hauled themselves on to the grass at the top. Looking out to sea, when she recovered her breath, Eliza saw that her plateau of rock was under water. In fact none of the rocks could be seen, the surge of water was lapping at the foot of the cliffs and the stretch of sand had disappeared.

Nathaniel looked at the scene before him in disbelief. It was only then, seeing that the tide had come in at such speed and reached such an unusual height that he appreciated the real danger they had faced.

'Edgar, thank goodness you were here as well,' he said shakily. 'I just don't know what has happened.'

'I came to warn you,' replied Edgar, shaking stones out of his sandals. 'There have been reports up and down the coast of unusual tides. Some people who live close to the beaches had to be warned and the revenue cutters have been busy. The lifeboat has been made ready in case of problems.'

'Why has this happened? Does anyone know?' demanded Barnabas.

'No one really knows but one theory is that there might have been an earthquake – remember one may have caused the cliff fall above Marietta Cove. There could have been another one out at sea.' Eliza shivered. 'And there was no warning,' she said.

As she looked at the grey sea and the grey sky, a break appeared in the clouds and a shaft of red sunlight shone through.

'There's the warning – just a bit late,' said Nathaniel cheerfully.

36

The bedraggled group presented themselves at the kitchen door to face Ewella's vocal concern. She observed that Barnabas was obviously exhausted, Eliza white-faced, her hair in lank strands, Edgar, his uniform covered in sand and dirt and Nathaniel minus his easel and painting. Only Kenwyn seemed untouched.

'Come in – come in!' exclaimed Ewella in alarm. 'What HAS happened to you all?'

'Did you not see the tide, Mistress Ewella?' Edgar said. 'I did tell Uncle Tobias that I was going to look for Barnabas and warn them all – '

'What are you talking about?' Ewella was impatient. Those who resided in Roscarne were well informed about tides. They should need no warning. Barnabas slumped into a kitchen chair.

'Ewella,' he began, in tones most unlike his usual brisk manner. 'Mr. Edgar came looking for us because the tides have been behaving strangely and posed a real danger to anyone down by the shore. Kenwyn and Caroline came back with the warning. Now we are all in need of refreshment and I think we should –'

At this point Eliza gave a little sigh and slumped to the floor, to general consternation. Ewella was galvanized into action.

'Perhaps you should put her on the sofa in the drawing room,' she instructed her brother. 'I shall tell Mrs. Adwyn to make hot drinks and meanwhile I shall find the sal-volatile, I know we have some somewhere. Barnabas, you and Nathaniel should change into dry clothes' – Barnabas, however, did not leave his wife's side until she opened her eyes.

Sometime later they were all gathered in the drawing room chattering excitedly about the tidal phenomenon on their shores. Uncle Tobias was insisting that earthquakes, albeit small ones, were common over the years. Grace, who had joined them, her silk dress frilled to the neck and chiffon scarf a reproach to the haphazard appearance of her sister and brother-in-law, demanded to know in detail what had happened and Nathaniel was pleased to enlighten her.

'No wonder you look so dreadful, Eliza. You should go to your bed.' Grace was not one to mince her words. 'Like a refugee from the Transvaal war!' Eliza's colour had not come back, there were shadows beneath her eyes and her hair had lost its usual glossy bounce. Concerned, Barnabas escorted her to her room and tucked her into bed, leaving hot milk by her side. Then he sat in one of the brocaded armchairs and watched while she sank into sleep.

His vigil was interrupted by Edgar who beckoned him out with urgency. 'Some mine captains are here,' he whispered. 'They are worried about safety, particularly in Wheal Rose and would like to see you.' Barnabas groaned. It should have occurred to him to check on the mines which had adits open to the shore.

'Please may I come with you, Mr. Barnabas? I may be of some help.' wheedled Kenwyn. 'You are exhausted still and I am not.' Barnabas nodded.

They accompanied Jack Smedley, the mine captain of Wheal Rose to the main shaft where they were met by a group of worried miners. It seemed that one of the younger lads was trapped in the lowest level of the mine after the hurried exit of his companions following water pouring into the adit from an exceptional high tide. This latter was not news to Barnabas and he was relieved to hear that the pumps installed by Seth before his departure were working well and the flooding was being gradually reduced. But in all the fuss and melee young

Jimmy Wendron had been left behind, trapped in a side-shaft as the others fled. It was surmised that he must have been injured and unable to keep up. His father was waiting at the pithead for him and alerted Jack Smedley that something had happened as his son had not surfaced. Barnabas demanded to know if anyone had been sent down to find the boy. But there was a further problem. The unexpected inrush of water had weakened one wall of the adit tunnel; some debris had apparently already fallen, indicating that the wall was in imminent danger of giving way altogether. Smedley looked really worried.

'They all want to go back an' search for Jimmy – but 'tis too dangerous'

'I shall go and find him,' said Barnabas quietly. 'This is my mine and my responsibility.'

He turned to the miners crowding round the head of the main shaft, Kenwyn hovering by his side.

'Lads – I appreciate that you wish to look for Jimmy. But you have families of your own who are waiting and worrying this very moment. I think that you should go back to your homes and take care of them. In any case, I believe that the noise made by a search party would risk further rockfalls and further casualties and I would never forgive myself if that happened. I intend to go down very quietly and I have the advantage of having explored the lower levels with the previous owner, Seth Quinn. Mr. Smedley – please see the doctor is called just in case.' Barnabas climbed into the cage which carried miners down the shaft and gave the signal for it to be lowered. At the last minute Kenwyn slid in beside him, ignoring Barnabas' protest. He knew how exhausted Barnabas was after his battle with the tide and he was determined to help Caroline's father. Contrary to orders most of the miners remained, clustered round the pithead, only a few drifting back to their homes. Jack Smedley knew better than to insist that they left.

Eliza arrived with Nathaniel to find a scene eerily reminiscent of the mine disaster so many years ago when she and Rose had rushed to find out what had happened to Barnabas and Seth and then stayed to care for all the families waiting for their men. The mine captain recognized Eliza and assured her that Barnabas would be quite safe; but he had gone down to look for young Jimmy Wendron who was missing.' The sympathetic glances of the men said otherwise. There was never a guarantee of safety down a tin mine and Eliza knew it. Nathaniel put his arm around his mother, finding her rigid and controlled.

'A young man went down with Mr. Barnabas to help him,' volunteered Mr. Smedley.

Time passed. Full night was upon them and lights sprang up, comforting pinpricks in the gloom. The mine doctor arrived but otherwise there was no movement. Surely there would be some news soon.

Hours later the creaking of the cage alerted everyone. Barnabas was coming to the surface. Would Jimmy be with him? They all crowded closer. And there was Barnabas carrying Jimmy in his arms. Kenwyn was carrying the lesser burden of a pickaxe and Jimmy's bag with his croust in it.

'He has a broken leg, I believe,' Barnabas said to the doctor.

'Mr. Trevannion carried me all the way,' piped up Jimmy. 'I was trapped behind lots of rock and stones which fell down and some fell on me so I couldn't move. Mr. Trevannion had to dig his way through to me. He was right brave.' There was a round of applause for Barnabas and for Jimmy who was making faces with the pain. A brief word with Jack Smedley and Barnabas turned to his wife and son, both weak with relief.

'I am so proud of you!' whispered Eliza.

'I would not have managed without Kenwyn,' said Barnabas. 'He helped me tunnel through to Jimmy and then

212

lift him out. I am so grateful and I shall see that Austol knows of his bravery.'

Back to Roscarne as dawn was breaking. Everyone in the family gathered in the drawing room to hear what had happened. Ewella had prepared a tasty supper for her brother and then shooed the children back to bed. Caroline saw Kenwyn off and soon only Uncle Tobias was left with Eliza and Barnabas. He was beaming.

'I am proud of you, Barnabas,' he declared. 'I shall write to Seth and Rose to tell them all about your courage. Now Eliza, you really must eat something. Brandy alone will not do!'

www.ingramcontent.com/pod-product-compliance
Lightning Source LLC
Chambersburg PA
CBHW070118260626

47160CB00004B/1524